WITH THIS LIE

A NOVEL

KAT SAVAGE

This is a work of fiction. Names, characters, places, and incidents either are the product of the author's imagination or are used fictitiously. Any resemblance to actual persons, living or dead, events, or locales is entirely coincidental.

First paperback edition February 2019

Graphic Design by Kat Savage of Savage Hart Book Services
Edited by Christina Hart of Savage Hart Book Services
Formatted by J.R. Rogue

ISBN: 9781796814101

www.thekatsavage.com

For the lost, the lonely,
the burned, the scared,
the ones surviving,
the ones who have fallen out of love,
& the ones too afraid to fall back in.

1

DANI

As a child, you learn how to give and receive love. In the absence of this teaching, you learn what is substituted. In my case, I learned to be callous. Some might even say calculating. I learned to be true to myself but trust no one else. I learned that everyone was a liar. These teachings make the notions of love and marriage nearly impossible to entertain. And while some may call what I experienced a trauma I need to heal from, I call it a way of life passed down to me as a means of survival. And I'm sure if I thought about it hard enough for long enough, I could begin to pinpoint the exact moment I decided these things were not in my future plans. No white wedding dress, no matching picket fence, and definitely no children. I think I was much younger than anyone would expect when making those kinds of lifelong decisions. The kinds of decisions people make well into their adult lives. Lately though, my mind revisits the same memory over and over again. Perhaps because it is part of what fueled my decisions. I think I've analyzed every detail of it trying to understand why it plagues me as much as it does.

I think I am about four years old. My mother leads me into my bedroom by the hand. She is smiling down at me through her long blonde hair she's curled with rollers and we stop in front of my closet. She is wearing one of her fancy lace nightgowns that she keeps in a special drawer in her dresser that I'm not allowed to open. She opens the closet door and spreads a blanket on the floor.

"Sit here, my love, my princess. This is your castle," she says to me.

I tilt my head at her, waiting for more explanation.

She hands me a small pink flashlight and my favorite coloring book and crayons. "Wait here for me until I come and get you. You'll be safe here. Okay, my love?"

I nod my head up and down vigorously. I don't want to disappoint her.

She kisses me on my forehead and shuts the closet door all the way until I hear it click.

I flick the flashlight on and prop it up in the corner of the closet.

I don't know how long I was in the closet. In my four-year-old mind, it could have been fifteen minutes or three hours. Looking back, my adult mind has processed that it was probably about an hour. My mother charged by the hour and rarely ever did a John want or need longer than that to get what he came for. My mother: the prostitute, the hooker. She always smelled like Virginia Slims and a cheap knock-off version of Obsession by Calvin Klein. It took me a few years to nail down that scent and sometimes I can still smell it in crowded restaurants or in groups of older women that walk by me on the street. Every time I do, I inhale the scent and exhale a fresh new load of recalled memories.

I roll over and stare up at the ceiling as I let my thoughts return to the present. At least it's an interesting ceiling. It's one of those snooty downtown lofts with exposed brick and pipes and ducts. My eyes trace over it all, wondering what the monthly bill on a place like this is. This guy is good for it, I'm sure of that.

I take a sideways glance at the man next to me. His back is toward me and he has a really cliché tattoo on his shoulder blade of some kind of tribal symbol. I imagine he probably got it in college and definitely doesn't know what it means, even all these years later. Probably picked it right off the wall in a fog of beer and double dares while chest bumping his frat brothers. One could only hope. I don't know for sure. We don't really talk much. It's not exactly what we prefer doing.

I feel him begin to rustle around under the blanket.

His legs kick away the sheet twisted around him and he sits up rather quickly. "I've gotta be out of here in an hour so you might want to get moving, sugar tits," he says.

Mark is your typical alpha male. Almost everything that spews from his mouth is annoying as fuck and sometimes even offensive. Scratch that. It's almost always offensive. I roll my eyes and begin stretching my arms up over my head. I don't have an issue bailing fast. I already got what I came for.

I stand and search the floor for my bra and feel his gaze burning a hole in my backside. "What?" I ask, looking over my shoulder at him.

He bites his lip and looks me up and down. "Damn. You're just so sexy. I can't control myself around you. Look what you do to me," he says, as he stands from the bed.

The man does have a nice body, I have to admit. There he is, his tent half-pitched. And like most typical alpha men, he's displaying it proudly. As if, as a woman, I just can't control myself at the sight of a stiff dick.

"Yeah, too bad there isn't any time." I feign a sigh. I am about as aroused as a damp towel at this point and not in the mood to stay. I find my clothes strewn about and start getting dressed.

"Maybe we have time for a little something," he says.

I hear his voice growing closer behind me and before I can respond, he presses his body into the back of mine—tent and all. He wraps his arms up around the front of me and grabs at my breasts. Lucky for me, I am skilled in the art of the slip away.

I spin around to face him, and back away at the same time, breaking his grip. "You'd better get your shower in while you can. Don't want to be late," I say, turning back around to finish dressing.

"Maybe we can meet for lunch? Bang a quick one out?" he asks, smirking, palming my ass cheek.

I finish putting my boots on and keep my back toward him. "Sorry, sugar. I can't today, as much as I love banging things out." I don't like to make these things too frequent. I need to spread Mark out over some time to recover from everything else I have to tolerate just to get the good sex.

I hear him huffing and walking off into the bathroom. He'll recover; I'm sure of it. I take my chance to slip out while he's in there. Part of me starts to wonder if putting up with him is worth what he provides. Sure, he's good in bed. But irreplaceable? No way. It's probably time for this Dani girl to start the ghosting process. He probably won't even notice.

Married men like Mark don't make a fuss about the side chick slipping away. There are probably ten more in line behind me. That's why he has the downtown loft close to work in addition to his family home in the suburbs half an hour outside the city limits. Men like him "work late" a hell of a lot more than they *actually* work late. Their wives don't care much, usually. They have their own lives, with "personal instructors" and weekly "ladies' nights" and no one says anything because the money does all the talking.

I put my earbuds in and start down the street, flipping through the music on my phone until I find the perfect walking home song. "Possum Kingdom" by Toadies fills my ears, and while I realize the song came out in 1994 and is sadly a quarter century old, this shit is still my jam. What can I say? I enjoy a wide variety of music and some of it is as old or even older than I am. At least it seems like most people say that. I've always wondered, though...if those music artists comfort us, who comforts them? This is exactly the kind of weird shit I think about when I'm walking home. I walk everywhere. I don't even own a car. I live right at the edge of downtown, close to everything including where I work, so I don't really see the point in having one. In this day and age, that makes me a very strange person to most people. They either assume I don't have a license or that I'm poor. Neither is the case.

I rub cocoa butter lip balm over my lips and wait for the light to change before crossing over Third Street to get to my block. When I make it to my red door, I pull my key out and notice my downstairs neighbor peeking through his window. Robert is an eighty-two-year-old man who refused to move when the area around him started to change. He's Italian and feisty and protective. He's pretty perfect. I walk up the two flights of stairs to my apartment and let myself inside. Aside from Robert, I don't really talk to any of my other neighbors. I think we all prefer it that way. Robert never seems frightened by the black nail polish I wear religiously or the tattoo on my leg or the fact that they probably all think I'm a lesbian because I've never had a man to my apartment. Everyone else in the building seems to think all this behavior adds up to me worshipping the devil or maybe even belonging to one of those awful Scientology groups. I don't really give a shit either way.

Robert once told me, "That's what color your fingers are after you die. I think they look like shit but they're your nails." Then he shrugged.

And that was the beginning of our perfect and lovely friendship. I remember I laughed for a few days about his initial reactions to me. I can always count on him for the truth, though, if nothing else. That's all a girl like me really needs anyway.

I throw my keys down on the table next to the door and walk to the kitchen. Glancing at the clock, I see I have three hours until I have to go to work. I crack my neck and knuckles, thinking about having a shower. I settle on a bath instead because I really need to soak everything in at this point. My phone buzzes and Mark's name lights up the front screen. I swipe to open the message and wish this kind of thing surprised me, but it doesn't. He'd sent me a dick pic. I will never understand entire generations of men thinking this is a swell fucking idea that will turn out well for them. Like, did I ask you for a picture of your dick? No. Didn't I just see your dick in person this morning? Yes. Do you think I fucking forgot what it looked like?

I shake my head and close my phone. You would think men would mature with age and this would only be a problem in the young ones, but that simply isn't the case.

I walk into the bathroom and exhale. Yes, my apartment is old and randomly placed and even looks a little run down from the outside. But the owners updated the interior. The bathroom is pretty magnificent. It was one of the reasons I chose this apartment to begin with. Under the small window sits a large soaking tub. The floors are new tile, and the light fixtures and cabinets are new and more modern than anyone would expect.

I turn the faucet on and let the water run over the back of my hand until the temperature is right. As the tub fills, I throw a bath bomb in and slip out of my clothes. When the water is high enough, I dip my left foot in and then submerge it completely, then my right. I sit down slowly, letting the water take me.

I don't have a lot of super feminine qualities. Or at least, I'm not the type of girl you see wearing a lot of dresses and getting their hair and nails done all the time. Not that there's anything wrong with that. I keep my hair in a long bob, which falls just below my shoulders. I keep my nails somewhat short and always paint them black. No other color is acceptable. I wear lip balm in place of lipstick or gloss. Vans and boots are my shoes of choice. I keep my makeup light and I have a few noticeable tattoos, the large one on my leg being the most noticeable in warm weather. Regardless, I relish bath time as if it were a spa. I even put a hydrating mask on my face during most bath time occasions, and today is no different. The woman in me loves face masks. I believe in pampering oneself frequently. I never had an issue with self-love growing up either. My mother taught me to always put myself first.

"You can only rely on yourself," she'd said time and time again.

My issue had always been loving others. Loving literally anyone else, really. I love my mom. I remember loving a boy in third grade, but it didn't last very long. Besides, I'm not sure love at that age counts.

The sheet mask peels off with ease and I lay it over the side of the tub. I notice the pruning of my fingers and cup water into my hands to gently rub my face, then wash my hair and body quickly before getting out. I pat my body enough not to drip and wrap my towel around my body. Once I'm in my bedroom, I pull the towel open and lie across the bed to stare up at my very boring ceiling. It isn't like the fancy loft ceiling. It is white and plain except for the small crack dissecting the center. I don't know how long that crack has been there or what caused it but it seemed like it just appeared one day out of thin air. Now, I've gotten into the habit of lying down to air dry and studying that particular crack. I've always air dried. Sometimes I even fall asleep completely naked and freshly bathed. Women everywhere understand this. Letting the under-boob dry in cool air is the only way to go. Spreading your legs sort of unladylike to let your thighs feel that same air. It is heaven. I don't understand people who don't do this.

I check the clock and still have almost two hours before work. Perhaps a nap isn't a terrible idea. I reach over and slide a pillow under my head. I fold the towel back over me and shut my eyes. I have a standard alarm set for half an hour before my shift starts so I know I'm safe. I start to drift off and think of my mother again, the way I did this morning. I think of my tiny castle, her frail paper hands, and her words to me.

I am beginning to miss her again.

2

LUCAS

"I THINK I LOVE YOU," SHE SAYS.

I stare back at her blankly. I snap my black rubber band against my wrist twice. Maybe if I don't move or acknowledge what she just whispered to me, it'll just go away. Maybe she'll say she was just kidding. Maybe she'll run out the door without saying anything else and I'll never see her again. Maybe if I wait long enough, I'll wake up and realize this is all just a nightmare and we will go back to normal. But none of those things are happening. It's not my luck. She is still staring at me and I am still silently staring back and fuck, this is about to get messy.

"But, baby, I told you it can't be like that. I'm a married man, and I'm sorry but that's not going to change," I say.

I wait for her to slap me across the face and storm out, but she doesn't. They rarely do. Though, if I were them, I would. Maybe they all want to in their heads but don't have the courage to actually do it. She starts to cry and fuck, I knew this was going to happen. I rub her shoulder.

It would be easier for both of us if she just slapped me. Anger is always an easier emotion to move through in these situations. Heartache is another beast entirely.

"I know. I know what you said but I just thought you should know and maybe it would change your mind," she says.

Sometimes, I'm a real dirt bag. But my decision to pretend to be married was really for everyone's sake. And I have to break it off with her now. We can't go back to the way things were before she said it. We can't erase this moment where it got too serious and pretend it didn't happen. I get up from her bed and start to get dressed. She probably isn't going to make this easy on me so I have to stay focused.

"Listen, Chelsea. We have fun. We do. I think you're great. You know that. But I just can't," I say. I look around for my shirt and find it draped over her desk chair. I don't remember how it got there last night but that's typical of most nights with Chelsea. I pull it over my head and then start to spin my fake wedding band around my finger and give my rubber band two more snaps.

She watches me search for my socks. She has a look in her eyes. Something akin to desperation, but if I was being nice, I could call it hope. Chelsea is tapped. We both have to move on and I hope for her sake she lets me go without much of a fight.

She dries under her eyes and sits up. "This is goodbye, isn't it?"

I drop my head down. God, I hate this part. She knows and I know and fuck me, why am I like this? It's for her own good, I tell myself. But really, this is about me. This has always been about me. My self-preservation. She'd hurt me eventually, and there's no way in hell I would let that happen to me again.

I kiss her on her forehead and tell her I'll see her around. Even though I won't.

I get out to the sidewalk and check my phone, finding a text from my brother, Elliott. I've been trying to get together with him to have drinks for a while now, regardless of the potential for a brawl. If I'm being real, I don't like my brother. I mean I love him, but we don't exactly see eye to eye on most things. That coupled with the fact that he's basically half the reason I'm so guarded and he really starts to contend for brother of the year. Maybe it's because we're only half-brothers. Or maybe the fact that his dad always treated me like shit had something to do with it. But my mother loved him, so I always just dealt with it.

My younger brother is a spoiled shit. I text him back, asking for a time and an address.

I get in my car and pull into traffic. I'm always so exhausted after something like this happens. Admittedly, this sort of ordeal has become a regular happening in my life. Once every few months or so. When the woman I'm seeing starts to want more.

Then I have to start all over again. It's getting old. I'm getting old. When I first started faking the whole being married thing, I thought eventually I would stop and maybe want to get back into dating with the purpose of settling down. That just hadn't happened though. I still have zero interest in putting myself out there to become a bug on some woman's windshield. I heard my heart go splat once and once is enough. No thank you to that torture.

I pull up to my apartment building and peer down the street. This section of the city is older but is being remodeled pretty quickly. I love the nuances of this area in Lexington. The streetlights are vintage, most buildings have exposed brick, and the streets even have cobblestone intersections. When people think about Kentucky, I'm sure they envision farmland and horses and that's totally true. But inside the city, you can't. I had secured this place long before the city started to take notice and "reinvent" it as a happening place, which meant I got it for a steal.

I check my mail on the way up and fortunately it's all junk. No real news is good news. I slide my key into the door and hear my neighbor's door open. I take a deep breath in preparation for what's to come.

"Hi, Lucas doll! Where have you been? I've been so worried. I tried to bring you some food over but you didn't answer your door. I was wondering if you could help me water my plants again?" she says.

Stella is a seventy-six-year-old widower whose grown children live out of state. The little woman stands no more than five-foot tall and honestly to say I think she's lonely would be a lie. I know she is. She's basically taken me in as her surrogate child, which is fine by me because both my parents are dead and Elliott's father is no father to me.

"Hi, Stella," I say. "I just spent a few days away. I'm okay, though. I can come water your plants in just a little while, if you still want?"

Most of the time, I'd make more small talk with her, tell a few jokes, really brighten up her day. But today, I just don't have it in me. She agrees and finally lets me shuffle into my apartment.

The inside is stale. When I went to stay with Chelsea for a few days, I told her it was because my wife was on a business trip. In reality, I cut off my central air, turned off all the lights, locked up my empty apartment, and drove over to her place. There is no one to come home to, no one to check in with, no one to ask where I've been. It's just me. Me and the trash I forgot to take out three days ago before I left. It now permeates throughout my small apartment and seeps deep into my nostrils as I approach the kitchen.

If ever you could call a place a "bachelor pad", mine would be a prime example. I bag up the garbage as I survey my kitchen counters. There is only an electric can opener and a toaster. I only have two magnets on my fridge and one is a bottle opener. I lift the bag out of the can and notice the dirty dishes on the coffee table. *Disgusting.* It seems I was sloppier than usual before I left. I look over at my vinyl collection. At least there is one thing in here to be proud of. I do take care of it. Not for myself really, but because my mother would have wanted it that way. Hell, I never have to bring a date back here so it isn't exactly like I'm concerned about the mess. So what if I leave the toilet seat up? So what if I don't do the dishes for five days? So what if I trim my beard over the sink? It's my place and no one is here to bitch at me for it.

The choices I've made probably don't sound great when spoken of, but they do allow a certain kind of freedom. Not to mention all the fun and none of the hassle. Let's face it. Society doesn't exactly set you up for a win. Humans aren't naturally monogamous. Like most animals, we crave the newness. And biologically speaking, there is some science behind "spreading your seed". I learned these lessons the hard way. One broken heart later, and I'm not on the sidelines watching people play the game anymore. I'm more of an all-star quarterback now. Not that I love my position. It's just how I survive.

I take the trash out and throw the bag over the edge of the dumpster and walk back inside. I think about sneaking back into my apartment without alerting Stella, but I don't want to stand her up. I need to get over to water her plants now since I won't be here later. I don't want to be late meeting Elliott. He texts me the address for a place I've never been to—apparently a favorite of his—and I know I'll need extra time to get there.

I stand in front of Stella's door for a full six minutes before I take a deep breath and knock. I know if I'm lucky, I'll be in and out of her place in about thirty minutes. The lady has a jungle's worth of plants, but what could really hold me up is her incessant need to worry about me settling down with the right woman. A nice woman. She'll ask me at least twice if I want kids and at least three times when I'm going to bring back a nice woman for her to meet. She'll even offer—for the hundredth time—to set me up with her single grand-daughter who "has a nice personality", which I will politely reject again. She has never even shown me a photo, and that's really all I need to know. If that labels me an asshole, then so be it.

It's exhausting, dodging all these questions. It's exhausting not having any new answers for her. Hell, I don't tell Stella how I operate. I don't tell most people how I operate. Maybe one or two people know and that is enough. The truth is, I'm not changing my ways any time soon. Probably ever. So I'll just keep dealing with the questions and offers.

I check my phone while I wait for Stella to answer the door. I can hear her shuffling around inside. There is a text on my front screen from Chelsea. "I miss you already." I don't even open it. Not responding is the best course of action now. It sucks, but ghosting is necessary.

I'm an asshole. I know it.

3

DANI

To be fair, I understand why my manager is always so pissed off when I arrive five minutes late for nearly every shift I'm scheduled to work. I live almost right above the bar (only one set of stairs over and up). In my mind, I can just walk out of my apartment at the exact time I should be at work but I always forget the amount of time it will take me to lock up, get down the stairs, and walk the one hundred feet to the little bar.

"You're late again, Dani," he says.

Calvin is a decent boss being that he is mostly good and mostly fair. I have no complaints and while I hate disappointing him, that disappointment lasts all of ten seconds each time and then I'm over it.

"I know, and as always I'm sorry but you love me and you forgive me and oh look there's a customer in need! Gotta go." I slip past him in the narrow kitchen hall and in behind the bar.

If I have learned one thing, I know Calvin will never chastise his employees in front of our patrons and we all take advantage of it. Sometimes I feel bad for him. Calvin managed to get us above-average wages, never has issues giving us time off, and even covers our shifts when no one else can. Someday I would make up for all my tardiness but today isn't that day.

"You're late again," Quinn says.

I turn to Flannigan's second-best bartender and study her perfect face. When I moved to this side of Lexington and started working here three years ago, Quinn was the first and only person I befriended. I couldn't say what it was about her that I attached myself to. We are polar opposites in so many ways. Perhaps she keeps me closer to level than I would be on my own.

"Shut up," I say. I tie my small black apron around my hips and start wiping down a messy area on the bar.

"Can you check my hair for me real quick? I feel like I'm getting a weird ripple right here," Quinn says, pointing to a section of the front of her perfectly straight hair.

If there was a ripple, it was imaginary. I pretend to take the matter seriously and stare at her hair for a second. "I think it looks fine." I smile.

"Are you sure? Maybe I should put it up," she says, stroking the supposedly rippled section of her hair over and over again. She studies her face in the mirror behind the rows of liquor behind us.

"I promise it's fine. We have a long night ahead of us, so if you could stop with your hair, that would be peachy." I roll my eyes at her in the most loving way.

WITH THIS LIE   19

"Okay, okay, you're right. I'm done," she says, still stroking her hair down.

Quinn is the epitome of perfection. No, I don't mean she is actually perfect. No person is. I mean she strives for it, craves it. She is a perfectionist in her marrow. But not in an annoying or vain way. Somehow, it is endearing and adorable. I think it's because you can sense the goodness in her, the kindness. She is always cheery, always polite. After all, perfection isn't about actually being perfect, it's about the act of perfecting.

I watch her for a few more moments. She's patting herself down as if she were a small bird attempting to unruffle her feathers. I nicknamed her "bluebird" a very long time ago, and am frequently reminded why.

I'll be here until close so I know I might as well settle in. That's a long nine hours from now. It's time to put my smile on and remind Quinn why I call her the second-best bartender here. Truth be told, I'm sort of an asshole, but I'm flirty. I like flirting and the men like me flirting. Many of the customers that frequent here are "happily" married men stopping by for some alcohol on their way home from work. Some come for their weekly "guys' night" while others are the type that don't even give their wives the decency of a text message letting them know they'll be late. Whatever their reason for being here, my job is to make sure they have a good time. I hate people for the most part, but I don't mind flirting my way to better tips. And besides, every married man who turns to putty in my hands at the bar is just another reminder as to why I'll never get married myself.

The dinner rush is slow and steady. We serve pretty good bar grub here. So while most are busy eating, it slows enough for me to leave Quinn for a moment and I step outside for a break. I use the alley in the back instead of out front because too many people know me and the last thing I want on my break is to spend it chatting with a customer.

I slide my cell out of my pocket and check my messages.

Mark: I'm seeing you later, right? I'll stop by your work and we can go back to my place?

Mark: Hello?

Mark: Dani??

God, he's needy. I can't imagine this Mark thing lasting much longer. I get the impression I'm a little more of a free spirit than he wants. He needs someone compliant, someone submissive. He needs someone who doesn't take up too much space and I make it my prerogative to take up a shit ton of space in any situation.

Me: Yeah, sounds good. See you later.

I don't even wait for a reply. I put my phone back in my pocket and rub my neck. Standing all day sure makes more than just your feet ache. I close my eyes and twist my head back and forth. I would take advantage of the jet sprayer in Mark's shower later. I feel my phone buzz inside my pocket and decide not to pull it back out. I don't have the energy for live texting at the moment. I will respond later, on my next break.

I go back in to relieve Quinn for her break and start welcoming in the after-dinner crowd. They are usually livelier, so we try to get our first breaks in before they're in deep. I am welcomed in by the familiar scent of Dan—a regular that wears his cologne too thick and his toupee too crooked.

"Hello, love," I say.

"How are you today, my darling?" he asks.

Dan is a kind man and as his bartender, I know all his stories. Dan was in the war. That's all he would say about it. I assumed he meant Vietnam. It's the only war that made sense. After that, he got a small place and married a pretty woman named Norma and they were together for nearly sixty years before she passed away. They didn't have any children. Norma couldn't. So they traveled a lot and saw the world together.

Now, Dan is pretty lonely. For his age though, he's in impeccable shape. He certainly isn't your average little old man.

"Oh, I'm fine, hun. Say, when are you going to let me fix you up with a good woman? Come on, Danny boy," I tease.

"Oh no, my darling. You know I only have eyes for you. Besides, everything is broken, no point in it now," he teases back.

I shake my head at him and get him another beer. He's the only man I know who was truly in love with his wife. He didn't even want another long after she was gone.

I wipe down the bar and refill drinks, and then I just listen. Listening is my favorite part of this job. As an avid observer, there is nothing like perking an ear up. The couple in the corner is fighting. Apparently, he's been making "fuck me" eyes at someone named Denise and he doesn't think his girlfriend notices. There are two men to the left of the couple who are gay but trying hard not to show off this fact, which I find kind of sad. Say it loud, sisters. Another drink or two in and the PDA would be abundant. There is a group of men toward the middle of the bar. They're partially blocking the service station where people sitting away from the bar come up and order. This is the most annoying type of customer. No regard for others. Maybe they're coworkers or old frat brothers. Who knows? A few had wedding bands and a few more had skillfully removed their wedding bands but you could still see the indentation and tan lines on their chubby little sausage fingers. No doubt there were two or three wives at home probably pregnant or taking care of a baby or multiple children.

The idea of being one of those women one day repulses me. I had seen too much, been a part of too much. I could blame my mother, but for what? Exposing the truth?

There is a middle-aged woman alone in the other corner of the bar. She's wearing a lot of gold jewelry and her lipstick is smeared. Her leopard pants coupled with her purple faux fur coat are a cry for attention. She shifts in her seat every few seconds and scans the room. She's on the hunt. I don't know her real name, but she looks like a Barbara. Barbara the cougar. Just then a man strolls up to Barbara and her eyes light up. *Go, Barbara.*

"How's it going?" Quinn asks as she steps in from her break.

"Same people, different day," I say.

"So, are you going to let me fix you up yet?" Quinn asks.

She'd been trying to set me up with her cousin almost the entire time I'd known her.

"Seriously? Again with this? You already know my answer," I say.

"Oh, come on, he's a really sweet guy," Quinn says.

"What kind of really sweet guy is single for three years then, huh?" I ask.

"Well, what kind of nice woman is single for three years?" Quinn sasses.

"That's your first mistake," I say.

"What?" she asks.

"Classifying me as nice when I'm anything but."

"I'm just saying…"

"And I'm just saying. I've designed my life, okay? It's this way for a reason. Thanks, but no thanks on the really nice guy," I say firmly.

"Fine," she says. Quinn holds her hands up in defeat.

She knows she lost. And she'll probably wait about three weeks before bringing it up again. I hate the notion that in order for a woman to be truly happy, she has to be with someone. My happiness hasn't been dependent upon another person since I was a child. And even then, it was never a man. My mother had been the only person in my life to have that kind of influence.

I float away from the bar for a moment, lost in my thoughts. My hands are there pouring drinks, but everyone's voices turn fuzzy.

I am about seven years old. My mother is leading me down the hallway again to my bedroom closet. I'm older now so I ask why.

"Oh, princess, the world is a dark place and sometimes you must hide inside your castle until it's bright again," she says softly. She runs her fingers through my hair and tucks it behind my ear.

I can smell her perfume. I can see her silhouette through her silk robe. I know this is when one of the men will come. One of the men who laughs so loudly I can hear it through the walls of my castle. One of the men who makes other noises. Who makes my mother make noises I don't understand yet.

"Okay, Mommy," I say, stooping down into the closet.

She hands me my small pink flashlight and my blanket from the end of my bed. I curl up with my book and flick the light on.

"Stay here until I come and get you, my princess," she says.

I nod as I always do and watch her disappear as the door closes, with a smile on her face and a look in her eyes I could never quite place. I know when she returns for me she won't smell the same and something about her smile will be off.

"Hello," an unfamiliar voice says, snapping me back to the present.

"Oh, hello. Sorry about that, what can I get for you?" I respond while pulling glasses up from the bottom rack. It isn't like me to greet a new customer without making eye contact, but I need a moment to collect myself.

"I'll just have a Heineken," he says.

"Coming right up!" I say, turning my back to him to get into the cooler. I pull the bottle opener from my back pocket and pop the top off. I turn to sit the beer in front of him and stop in my tracks. Whoever he is, wherever he came from, he is next-level gorgeous. There's a lot of things I can play cool about, but a beautiful man isn't one of them. I have weaknesses and I am staring one of them in the face.

He smiles a very relaxed, natural-looking smile. "Hello again."

I gulp, slowly sitting his beer down onto the cardboard coaster in front of him. All I can hear in my head are the lyrics to "House of Cards" by Radiohead.

"Oh, hello there." I give my best fake bartender smile. The same crappy smile I give a hundred patrons a night.

"That's not your real smile, is it?" he asks, raising his eyebrow.

Wow, calling me on my bullshit early.

He must notice my surprise because he chuckles. "I'm only kidding," he says.

I return a nervous laugh. "Can I get you anything else?"

His eyes search around the bar. "I'm actually just waiting for my brother. I don't see him here yet so I'm good for now, thank you," he replies.

I nod at him and shuffle back a couple of steps.

Someone yells, "Excuse me, miss?"

And I redirect my attention to assist them and some of the

other patrons, all the while stealing glances of him from the corner of my eye.

My favorite game to play with myself to pass the time is to create back stories for the people I run into. He has a ring on—of course—but he doesn't really look like your average married man. He definitely doesn't have the suburban dad bod or terrible husband haircut. His dark brown hair and beard look soft and touchable. *A very touchable beard.* His eyes are a beautiful blue-green. He seems taller despite being in a seated position. And lean, like a swimmer. Swimmers' bodies are delightful. I try guessing his name in my head. *Garrett? No. Andrew? Nope. Daniel? Nu-uh.* I mindlessly wipe the counters in front of me.

This is exactly the sort of man my mother would tell me to run from, to keep a distance from. Men like that—the beautiful, unobtainable type—are exactly the type to hurt you. A beautiful man can break you down before you ever know what is happening. One moment you're Kelly Clarkson's "Miss Independent" and the next you're Pink's "Just Like A Pill". It spirals out of control so fast, you don't even recognize yourself and you're lovesick all over the sidewalk and your favorite pair of boots. *No way, man. Not me.*

I glance over at the exact moment he tries to wave me over and I make my way to him. I swallow big again. "What can I get ya?" I ask.

"Well, turns out my brother is standing me up, which is not a big surprise, so I'll have a shot of Jameson and the check, please." He forces a small polite smile past his visible disappointment. His eyes are sad.

It makes me sad for him. "Well, I'm sure he's got a good reason, right? I'm sure you'll catch up soon."

"Thanks, but probably not. We haven't seen each other in eight years, even though we live in the same city," he says.

"Oh, that sucks." I grab a shot glass from the rack and turn it over in front of him. I spin around, grab the Jameson from the shelf, tip the bottle up, and fill the shot glass all the way to the brim.

"Whoa now," he says, chuckling.

"Seems like you could use it," I say, smiling.

He nods, taking the shot in his hand. Some spills down his thumb as he hoists it in the air and knocks it back. He doesn't even flinch.

That's hot. I have a thing for men who can handle the hard stuff.

He pulls his thumb up to his lips and licks the droplets from the back of it.

Christ on a cracker. I clear my throat.

"Thanks," he says.

He is staring at me now, making entirely too much eye contact for my comfort. For anyone's comfort really. No one does that anymore. No one just looks at someone, looks through them.

"So, the check," he says, breaking the silence.

"Don't worry about it," I say. "It's on the house." And what I mean by that is I will pay for it out of my tips. I do that sometimes for sad girls that come in. Sometimes they've just been dumped. Sometimes, like this man, they've been stood up.

He is smiling again, though. "Well, thank you…"

"Dani Monroe," I say.

He nods. "Thank you, Dani."

"You're welcome…"

"Lucas Kane," he says.

"You're welcome, Lucas," I say, smiling a rare but genuine smile. It isn't often one is provoked from my lips but Lucas just stole one and I am not complaining.

"I'll see you around," he says, stepping off his stool and turning away to leave.

I watch his triceps flex as he pushes off the bar. I watch the dimple form in his right cheek as he glances back. I watch him glide between people and out the door and into the night. Regardless of his parting words, I doubt I'll ever see him again. It happens now and again. I happen upon a truly entertaining specimen and then they walk out the door and I never see them again. It's a real bummer, but perhaps I'm only meant to have these tiny little moments with them and that's it.

I start to think about all the people who have disappeared from my life. Sometimes with a goodbye, sometimes under a cloak of darkness, and sometimes without even looking in the rearview at what they left behind. I've been destroyed by too many goodbyes with no one nearby to build me back up. People don't stay. We are nomadic at our cores. I lived in four different apartments in the four years before my current one. I never switch cities because I'm tied down here, as much as I don't want to be. As much as I wish I didn't have to be. I can't leave this place.

So I stand here, while all the world moves around me,

while all the people go on from this place and never look back. And I watch them. Usher them on. Maybe that's what I'm meant to do.

4

LUCAS

I step out onto the sidewalk and into the changing air. The sun's gone down but the city is still all lit up. I bet I couldn't see the stars even if I was standing on the tallest building. I inhale slowly and find myself still smiling from the brief interaction with that firecracker of a bartender.

She looked like she could be fun. To my surprise, I found myself stealing glances of her all night. She was perky. Her blonde hair bounced around in unison with her body as she ran back and forth serving people. She smiled those genuine, happy-to-be-here smiles at everyone. A couple of times though, I caught her when she'd drifted away to somewhere else the way she was when I first arrived. Her face changed. It became like glass, like if she let a tear fall, it would shatter. People like her have monsters under their beds and skeletons in their closets, and a suitcase full of demons at the door to pick up on their way out. People like her bail. I know, because I've fallen for that type before. So many people inside one body.

I check my phone for any word from my brother. Elliott is

a real dick. In all my life, the only person I've ever been stood up by is a person that's supposed to be my goddamn brother. Well, half-brother anyway. I should have known. He's never really been a brother to me. He's dicked me over on more than one occasion. I just thought we could move to a place of healing after all these years. He wounded me. And all I've been trying to do is get past that, but he isn't helping matters.

I turn back toward the windows of the bar to see if I can steal one last look at her. Dani. I keep wondering if it's short for Danielle. I'm tempted to go back in and ask. I'm tempted to go back in and ask a dozen questions starting with what her phone number is. If she says no, I'll be disappointed. If she says yes, I'll probably still be disappointed. I look down at my left hand. If she were the type of woman who wanted to keep company with a married man, I'd be a little sad.

I turn back away. Perhaps the version of her in my mind, the one with gaps I fill in myself, is the best version in this situation. No need to spoil it.

I walk to my car and get in. I check my phone again. Nothing. I should go home and shower again just to rid myself of this disappointment and curiosity. No good can come from either. I make the short drive to my apartment and head toward my door only to be met by Chelsea.

The poor girl is sitting on my stoop, looking down at her phone. She hasn't seen me yet and I wonder if it's too late to back up. I pause for a moment and when I do, her head pops up.

"Lucas," she says.

It isn't a question or a statement. It sounds like a prayer, or perhaps what I think a prayer would sound like. I don't really have a lot of firsthand experience with that.

"Chelsea? What are you doing here? How do you even know where I live?" I ask, afraid to hear what she's about to say.

"I just thought…I thought maybe I could come here and make you see we are meant to be together," she says.

I look down the sidewalk left and right and realize I need to shift into character. "Chelsea, you can't be here. My wife is upstairs. You can't do this," I say, still wondering how she got here.

"I followed you home the last time you left. I sat here and watched for a while but I left before I saw your wife. I was too afraid. But come on, I mean there's a reason you were in my bed. There's a reason you don't stay here. You're unhappy and I can make you happy. I can. I know I can."

I shake my head. *Wow.* This doesn't happen very often but when it does, I feel like total shit. Chelsea is just a woman. She fell for a man who doesn't want any part of falling. And now she's going to be sad and I never wanted that either. I can see the pain and hope in her face. I can see what it's going to do to her either way. I can drag this out to pacify her, to make her feel better for now. Or I can rip it off like a Band-Aid and get the crushing over with and she can begin to heal now. Either way, it still paints me an asshole. Either way, no one gets what they want.

"Chelsea. You knew what this was when we started. You knew what this was way before we got here. You know I can't be with you. It's complicated." I sigh.

She is fidgeting with the bracelet on her left wrist, shaking her head back and forth in disbelief. "I just don't understand why you don't leave her," she snaps. The desperation in her voice quickly turns to anger, to frustration.

"I just can't, Chelsea. We've been through this. It would destroy her. She's unstable," I say, making my fake wife out to be the problem. God, that's about as low as I can get. I'm not even nice to my fake wife. How the fuck would I treat a real one?

"That's fine, I get it. Men like you string good women like me along for the sake of a crazy woman who obviously doesn't give you what you need. That's fine. I can find better, you know? I can. And I will." With that, she turns on her heel and walks away with extra sway in her hips.

It's the kind of walk a woman pulls out when she definitely wants regret to sink into you. I feel some, just not for the reasons she probably hoped for.

I stand there, rubbing the back of my neck. I close my eyes and exhale. I look up at the dark windows of my building, glad we hadn't attracted any of my nosey neighbors to gawk. I walk up the stoop and stick my key in the door. I start to wonder if Chelsea is the type to push things, to make things harder. Hell, she had followed me home once already, staked my place out. Would she go further?

I shake the thoughts from my mind and let myself into my apartment, heading straight for the kitchen to pour myself a Jameson. At this point, I need it to sleep.

I check my messages. Nothing from my brother. *Figures.* I don't know why I ever expected it to get better between us. It had never been good, in spite of how much I hoped for it. Maybe it's because we had different fathers. Maybe we just inherited different shit from them that made it impossible to be close. Truth be told, I'm not sure I ever felt a bond with him. All I remember is trying make his dad like me, make him be proud of me, and nothing ever worked. I remember him treating Elliott better than me. He was the type of guy who wasn't good at treating a kid who wasn't his as his own. I figure I'll never actually know the real reason me and Elliott aren't close, but forming my own conclusions helps a little. His father being one of them. It at least gave me options. Perhaps if I keep trying, we'll get there. Hell, maybe if I keep trying, we will at least get to a place where he doesn't fucking stand me up.

I sit on the end of my bed and fall back. I have half a mind to fall asleep just like this, feet on the floor and all. But I manage to shimmy up to my pillow, grateful it's the weekend and there's no alarm to set or place to be. I can just sleep until I feel better about the mess I've made out of my life. I didn't know it was possible to feel this lost. I had the map in my hand and couldn't bring myself to use it. I roll over on my side, pulling the gold band from my finger and placing it on my nightstand.

With this one small gesture, I unpack all my lies. It's easier to fall asleep like that.

5
_____

DANI

I can't say I'm surprised by what is happening right now. Of course Mark didn't actually stop by my work like he said he would. Of course he texted me saying he was unable to make it. Of course I'm walking to his place late at night now to meet him there instead. Of course I can't actually stay all night because he has to get back to his actual life.

So what am I stopping by for? A fucking booty call. A quick ass booty call that I have to walk home from afterwards. God, I'm an idiot.

I make the trip to his building pretty quickly, and buzz myself in. I shake my head the whole way up and ring the bell in anger. I cross my arms while I wait.

"Hey baby," he says, smiling, as he opens the door.

It's his cheese eating, I'm-the-fucking-man grin and it disgusts me. I don't remember it always being like this with him.

"Hey," I say coldly.

"What's wrong?" he asks, as if nothing had gone wrong.

"Seriously? How can you even ask me that with a straight face?"

He scratches his chin and shrugs his shoulders. "So you want to do this or what?"

Wow. Fucking wow. He clearly doesn't give a shit and that question was the last straw for me. "You know what, Mark? No. No, I don't want to do this. I don't want to do this anymore," I say, arms still crossed.

"I'm sorry, what? You're rejecting me? You're breaking this off with me?" he asks.

"Yes. I am."

He scratches his chin again. "Listen, Dani, I don't know who the fuck you think you are, but women don't tell me no. I'm fucking Marcus Stone. You got that, bitch? You don't break up with me, I break up with you. And you know what, I'm not fucking done with you." He steps toward me, making fists with both hands at his sides.

I stand there in shock at what he just said. I don't even know how to respond. Men like him think they can say whatever they want and we just need to obey, need to take it for what it is and step back in line. I don't fucking think so.

"Listen Mark, I'm going to just go ahead and ignore the fact that you just said some stupid ass shit and I'm going to leave. You have a good night and a good life," I say, turning to open the door.

Mark's hand flies past my face and slams the door back shut. He pushes me face first up against the door and pins me there, his body pushing uncomfortably against mine. "I don't think you heard me, Dani. I'm not done with you," he says, as he runs his hands into my hair and jerks my head back.

"Let me go, Marcus," I call out. I never called him Marcus until now. I feel him rubbing himself against my backside, taunting me.

"I don't think I will," he says, sliding his hand down my side and around between my legs.

"I'm asking you nicely to think about what you're doing and let me go before it's too late," I say, calmly. I know better than to panic or show fear in this kind of situation. That's what he wants.

"I don't think I'll regret what I'm about to do." He shoves his face into the crook of my neck to kiss and bite.

He leaves me no choice. I lower my arm and send my elbow back into his stomach as hard as I can. He drops his arm and head down to cup his stomach and I send another elbow back straight across the bridge of his nose. He screams out in pain and cups his face as he falls to the ground. I kick him for good measure and open the front door. I turn to him for just a moment.

"Don't you ever think about touching me ever again. Lose my number, you fucking asshole." I slam the door shut behind me. This will be the last time I ever see him. I'll let the staff at work know he's banned from the bar now and that'll be the end of that.

I get out to the sidewalk and take in a few deep breaths of fresh air. Goddamn that feels good. I don't know why I ever tolerated his entitled ass to begin with. I can already feel my phone buzzing in my pocket and I'm sure he's sending me some very colorful texts.

I ignore them all the way home, carrying my mace and keys between my fingers. That's one thing about being assaulted or nearly assaulted. You're a little on edge after. I haven't been seeing Mark for that long but something tells me he's the vengeful type. I could just picture him trying to catch up with me and seek out some sort of revenge.

I make it to my building without incident and hurry in. I'm not too frightened to defend myself, but I certainly don't want to spend any more time than I have to in a vulnerable spot. I lock up my apartment and see my hands shaking with both adrenaline and fear for the first time tonight. I walk into my bedroom and strip out of my clothes, putting on a long t-shirt and opening my closet door. Moving a few things out of my way, I sit down and lean against the wall. After a few short, jagged breaths, I begin to cry.

For as long as I could remember, anytime I needed to cry, I sought out my closet. I never cried outside of a closet. The world is no place for softness, for vulnerability. It will destroy it. It will take a soft thing and bend it until it breaks. The world is no place for tears or hearts. I leave that all in here, in the closet. This is the only place it's ever felt safe to do so.

I close my eyes and let it all out on the floor of my closet, like a child, like a frightened small thing. I am angry with myself. I am angry with Mark. I don't let men make me feel this way. I don't let men make me feel any way, good or bad, for that matter. I have to regain composure. I will sit here until I can leave this all here behind me. That's what the closet is for. Still, after all this time, my tiny castle is where I leave all my softness.

My eyes begin to dry and I picture my mother's face smiling at me, cupping my chin like I am five again. The problem with losing your mother before you're done needing her is that your mind begins to manifest false memories. You start to inject her in places she never was. And the problem with life is, you're never done needing her. Foster care taught me a lot. I didn't suffer the bad experiences I know some others did. Sure, I bounced in and out of homes. No place became permanent. I eventually aged out. But it wasn't the worst thing. Nothing though, nothing had taught me how to stop missing her. And no one would understand the real reason she was gone.

I wipe the last few tears from my face and stand up. I stare at my phone for a moment and think about reading the texts from Mark but decide it isn't worth it. I'm ready for bed and whatever he says can wait until morning to be erased.

I lie down and replay the evening one last time. Mark had been a nightmare. Work had been way too busy. Nearly assaulted. Caught off guard by the illustrious Lucas. *I wonder if he goes by Luke?* Stupid Mark. Stupid, stupid Mark. Who even acts like that? *Prick.* I was looking to end things with him soon anyway but he certainly helped the cause tonight.

I don't want to think of him while I fall asleep. I shift my thoughts back to Lucas. His smile. His dimples. His hair.

He is too pretty not to think about while drifting off. Maybe I'll wake up tomorrow and all this will have never happened. I can't get that lucky in life. I know one thing. At least I'm free again. These days though, freedom feels a lot like loneliness.

6

LUCAS

I WAKE ABRUPTLY TO THE SUN SHINING IN ON ME, CAUSING me to sweat. I check my phone and I see that I fucking slept until eleven. That's lunch time for some people. I guess I really needed it. The night did end on an intense note after all.

I make my way to the kitchen, to the coffee. I slept half my Saturday away. *Now what?* I hate that I always feel guilty for sleeping. It feels like wasted time, and apparently as an adult, you're not allowed to do that. It makes no sense to me. Maybe I will take the day to just be by myself. Maybe go for a run or drive out of the city. I'm not awake enough to make that decision just yet.

I grab my coffee and slump into the living room and onto the couch. I stare at my mother's record player. I wasn't much for listening to music myself, but she wanted me to have it when she died so I held onto it along with her entire vinyl collection. I never actually play it. It's a shame really. I'm sure there are others who would enjoy it much more than I am. I flip through some vinyl records in a box next to me. I don't even know most of these bands.

I check my phone as I sip my coffee. Elliott still hasn't replied to me. I snap my rubber band against my wrist. Not surprising. We haven't seen each other in so long. He doesn't know I've cut all my hair off or that I have a beard now. Or that I've put on several pounds of muscle. I'm not the chubby kid I was back then. Hell, he probably wouldn't even recognize me on the street. But if I know him, and I do, he won't look any different. He will still be the same, polished priss he always was. I stop my thoughts there. No need to dwell on something that will never change.

It feels like a walking day. Every once in a while, I take a free day and I walk around the city. I meander up and down streets for miles, nearly getting lost. Sometimes I walk for hours. Yeah, that sounds like a good plan. It will give me time to reflect on my thoughts, and I won't be a shut in. Sometimes getting lost is the best way to find the answers.

I put on some jeans and a t-shirt along with some shoes comfortable enough to do a lot of walking in and head out. I turn right and just start walking with no intention and no direction in mind, ready to see where the day takes me. I like to observe people as I walk, the way they interact with others. I notice a woman getting out of what I can only assume is an Uber ride. I notice a business man on his cell phone, late to a meeting no doubt. He narrowly misses running into a woman coming out of a shop. Men like that have no sense of an outside world, no sense of others with just as complex lives as they have. These are my least favorite people.

Two kids are playing at the edge of the park on the corner

and I decide to cut through there. The city did a good job of nestling parks throughout, with mature trees and pleasant paths. They almost make you forget you are actually in a concrete jungle. I walk the longest path, taking me from one side of the park to the other, several blocks over. I come out the other side near a café I've never tried so I decide to stop in for lunch. Considering I slept so late, I'm skipping right over breakfast which is so unfortunate.

I take a seat in the corner booth next to the window so I can watch people pass by on the street. I like watching men in particular. Not because I'm harboring any latent sexual curiosities, but because I wonder what they are like. I wonder if they have families. I wonder if love screwed them over too. I envy the ones that look happy. I imagine they have wives and children and houses they've worked for. I imagine they didn't fuck up their lives like I did by being too frightened to "get back out there" as my friends call it. With just one continuous lie, I managed to completely restructure my entire life.

"What can I get for you?" the waitress asks, breaking my thoughts and stare. I snap my rubber band and look up at her.

I shift in my seat and grab the menu. "I just need a few minutes, but can I get a water with lemon?"

She nods her head and turns on her heel. I stare down at the menu and realize I'm not really that hungry but probably should eat if I plan to walk the day away. I begin to mindlessly read each item and its whole description like I don't know what comes on a BLT all of a sudden. This is the sort of thing I do when I'm being indecisive.

"Hello," a familiar voice says, just beyond the menu.

I pull the menu down from my face to see who has interrupted my thoughts this time. I glance up to see an even more familiar bouncy blonde bob and a head tilted sideways at me.

"Well, hello there." I smile at her.

"Do you remember me?" she asks.

"Of course I do. Dani, right?" I pretend to have forgotten a little, so as not to appear so eager. This is the type of thing you have to keep in check.

She smiles again. "That's right. So do you live around here?" she asks, looking out the window in different directions.

"Not so fast. Do you remember my name?" I tease, smiling mischievously.

"Lucas," she says, raising a hand to one hip.

"Okay, okay, I'm just checking," I say. "And to answer your question, sort of. If you were to walk through that park over there, I'm on the other side of it. Do you live around here?"

"The bar where we met, the one I work at, is just about two blocks up from here."

I look out the window, up and down the street. "Oh, I guess I hadn't realized," I say. "Small world, huh?"

"And getting smaller," she says.

She's still standing and it's getting to the point where I need to say something. "So, would you like to join me?" I ask, gesturing to the seat across from me.

There's a little hesitation in her face and she looks around.

I wait for just a few moments longer.

"Sure, why not?" she finally says.

"Don't sound so excited," I say.

"I could pretend for you, if you want?" she says, teasing back.

"Ouch. You pull no punches," I say.

She sits across from me and picks up the other menu.

I pretend to look over it even though I decided what I wanted before I ever came in and started reading the damn thing. "So what will you have?" I ask.

"Probably a salad," she says.

"Why?" I ask.

"Why what?"

"Why probably a salad? Is it because you're one of those girls who likes salad or is it because some moron told you that you were fat at some point?" I ask.

"Wow. Now who's not pulling any punches?"

"I can be blunt sometimes. I apologize," I say, sitting my menu down in front of me.

"It's okay. I like it," she says. "It's a bit refreshing, given humanity's current climate."

We both laugh and settle into a bit of silence before the waitress returns.

"I noticed you had company, so I brought two waters with lemon. Hope that's okay?" she asks, looking down at Dani.

"It's perfect, thank you," Dani says.

The waitress takes our orders and walks away and we are facing the silence again.

"To answer your question, both," Dani says. "I genuinely like salad. And also, at some point in my life, men have been mean to me."

I nod, admiring her complete honesty and vulnerability in this moment. There was nothing to tease about there. "Thank you for your honesty," I say.

"You would be the only one thanking me. No one else seems to actually appreciate honesty the way they say they do. Everyone wants the truth, but only if it fits into their box, if it fits their needs. If it doesn't, well, then you're not being honest, you're being a dick. I guess I just fail to see the difference." She shrugs.

Wow. In all my life, I'm not sure I've met someone who spoke this kind of honesty. It isn't just refreshing, it's sexy. "You might not believe me, but I completely and totally agree with you," I say.

She smiles and nods in confirmation.

Our booth falls silent for a few minutes, perhaps because neither of us know what to say next. Perhaps because we are both trying not to say too much. It isn't as awkward as I imagine some encounters to be. It's sort of nice, actually. More natural.

"So you're married?" she asks, gesturing down at my ring.

Fuck. Full on panic mode is now settling in. I can't exactly back up now. Fuck. "Umm, yeah, I am actually," I say. I snap my rubber band. Curse this stupid ring and curse my habitual putting it on when I leave the house and curse me for being such a dick.

"Happily?" she asks, raising an eyebrow and smirking.

What? No way. Not her. Really? If I knew anything by now, it's how a woman reacts to news that you're married but doesn't actually give a shit and would totally pursue you anyway. And this was that. And I didn't expect that. "You caught me. No, not really. It's been very hard recently," I reply, playing my part as usual.

"Why don't you just leave her, then?" she asks.

This is always the next question. I always give the same answer. "I'm not sure, really. A part of me really loves her, you know? A part of me tries to hold onto the memories of what we were before this, and I like to believe we are capable of being those people again, capable of having what we had again." This always gets them right in the heart.

But Dani just nods her head. She sits back all the way against the booth seat and folds her arms in front of her. "I call bullshit," she says.

Well, I can't say that's ever happened until now. 'I'm sorry?" I ask quickly.

"You heard me. Bullshit," she says.

I stare back at her in confusion. "I'm not sure what you mean," I say.

"Well, the way I see it, one of two things is really happening. You're either still in love with her and actively working to get back to the happiness you once shared. Or you don't love her, and you're actively trying to leave. But, since you're not doing either of those, and you're sitting here with me, I say you like things just the way they are." She tilts her head and raises her eyebrows at me.

Fuck. I can't say I've ever had someone call me out like this. I'm not even sure what to say to her in response at this point. She's still just sitting there waiting for me to make sense. I can deny it, or I can risk it. Decisions, decisions. "You caught me again," I say. "The truth is, we've grown so far apart. I miss affection. Sometimes I look for it somewhere else. And I'm sure she's doing the same."

Dani seems at least a little satisfied with my answer, nodding her head again in my direction. "So is that what this is? You looking elsewhere? Is that why you invited me to join you?" she asks.

I hesitate. Here is the moment. "No, no. Well, I mean, maybe," I say, fidgeting with the silverware at the edge of my napkin. I look up into her eyes. I can tell she's contemplating my words. I can tell she's thinking hard on it. I don't know what kind of woman she is. And I'm afraid I'll get what I want, which isn't what I want. I want her to be better than that. I want to know she's a good, decent woman.

"I'm going to tell you something I've never told anyone," she says. "And I don't know why I'm going to do it, but for some reason, I don't want you to paint me a certain way when there's more to it than what's on the surface. Okay?"

"Okay," I say.

"I only date married men. And it's not because it's fun to be bad, or because I like it in some strange way. And it's not because I'm looking to wreck a home. I do it for security. Because I don't want love and I don't want 'the real thing' and I don't want to get hurt. And dating married men makes that easier. Married men never leave their wives, even when you ask them to, and married men aren't there to catch feelings. They just want to have fun. And that's all I want. And that's it," she says.

I wait for a moment, to see if there's more but that really is it, and I'm left a little speechless. I comb back over her words in my mind and think about how wounded she must have been in her life to arrive on this path, how painfully someone must have hurt her to be so shut down toward love. But what's worse, is I understand it on a level she'll never know about. I understand it in my core. She's the same as me in terms of self-preservation, which makes me wonder if I should tell her my secret.

"I get it," I say. And I could choose to tell her the truth about me now, but then I'll never have a chance to get to know her. She'd shut us down before we ever started because then she'd know I'm not actually married. Or, I could keep pretending to be married. I could keep pretending so I can get to know this strange and beautiful creature that grows even more so with each minute. And the inevitable end? I couldn't worry about that now. All these things eventually end. I would have to deal with that later.

"You do?" she asks.

"I really do, actually. After my first fiancé left me, I shut down for a long time. I didn't let anyone in. And then, well, I guess I just healed little by little as time went on," I say.

"And then you found it?" she asks.

"Yeah, I did," I say. I snap my rubber band again.

She smiles at me. Her face is almost hopeful. "That sounds nice. I'm glad you found it," she says.

And I know she's genuine. Silence falls over us again and

our food gets delivered. We each look down at our plates and back up at each other.

"So, now what?" I ask.

"Now, we eat," she says, picking up her fork.

I nod. Eating is simple. I can eat. I pick up my BLT and take a bite. I watch her drizzle dressing onto her salad and mix it around with her fork. I see her cross her legs at the edge of the table and see a tattoo on her thigh peeking out from her shorts. I want to ask what it is but I don't want her to know I'm staring at her legs so I decide against it.

"Where does your wife think you are when you're...occupied?" she asks.

She's so forward. No one ever asks these things.

"Well, it depends on the time and day. Sometimes I'm working. Sometimes I'm hanging out with friends. Sometimes I'm having alone time," I reply.

"And she never questions you?" she asks.

"Not usually. Like I said, she doesn't seem to care," I say.

Dani nods. "Do you want to come see me later at work?" she asks.

Even with the mouthful of food, I start to nod and try to mumble a "yes" through the chewing.

She laughs and I like the way it sounds.

"What time should I be there?" I ask.

"My shift starts at eight and I get off at midnight. Just a short one tonight to cover for someone else. Maybe if you show up before I get off you can find me behind the bar.

Then we could hang out after I get off, if you want?" she asks.

"Definitely," I say. I'm eager and she knows it.

She smiles and I'd like to do more things that make her smile.

We finish eating and walk outside onto the sidewalk. As we're standing there, she pulls out her headphones.

"What kind of music do you listen to?" she asks.

"I don't really listen to music," I reply.

Her jaw drops and she looks almost wounded.

I shift my eyes back and forth and I don't know what I've done wrong.

"What do you mean you don't really listen to music? How is that even possible?" she asks, dismay in her voice.

"I mean…I don't know, I just never got into it," I say. By this point, she's looking at me like I'm an alien. I'm not sure what else to say so I wait for her to say something.

"Okay, okay, this is fine. I'm not freaking out but you should know this is a big deal and you're really weird." She laughs. "But that's okay because I can fix it."

"You can fix it?" I ask.

"Yes, I can fix you, weirdo." She giggles. "I'll see you later. I obviously have work to do."

"I'll see you later then," I say, walking back toward the park.

I check back over my shoulder to see her bouncing down the pavement, headphones in, completely unaware that she's so unbelievably intriguing. I turn back and start my walk through the park. This is the exciting part. The newness of something is always so fun and full of wonder. There's a lot of laughing and sparks and…hunger. I'm ready for it.

I'm definitely ready for it.

7

DANI

THIS MAY BE A BAD IDEA. BEAUTIFUL MEN ARE ALWAYS A BAD idea, actually. My headphones are in and I'm listening to "Slow Down Love" by Louis the Child but my mind is still back half a block. I glance over my shoulder and see him still watching me walk away. But how could a man just not be into music? How could any person not be into music really? Clearly, he needs a musical education and if I do one thing during our time together, however long it lasts, I will give it to him.

I glance over my shoulder again but he's out of sight. I still have a few hours before work and I plan to use it wisely. I need to run some errands and maybe spend some extra time getting ready for work. I mean, I sort of have a reason to look a little extra cute, right?

I make it up to my apartment and head for the closet. What do you wear when you want to look cute for someone but don't want them to know you're trying to look cute for them? Decisions, decisions. It's still really warm out so I pull out a pair of black high-waisted cut-off jean shorts. These say, "look at my ass", but also, "I just threw these old things on, no big deal". Perfect. I'll just pair it with a simple tank top and a push-up bra and that should do the trick.

My phone buzzes from across the room and I roll my eyes because I know it's Mark. He's been texting me every hour. First, they were vague apologies. Then, they sort of shifted into demands. As if, simply because he offers the apology, I am obligated to accept it? No, cupcake. That's not how it works. There's no rule about that. I think as we grow up we are taught that accepting apologies and forgiveness is the polite thing to do, but that's such garbage. I am not obligated to accept or forgive simply because it's what the other person wants, or what would make them feel better. You know what would make me feel better? Giving him another elbow to the nose. He should be thankful all I'm doing is ignoring him.

I lay out my clothes for later and grab my phone. I bypass the messages and go straight to the music. I start a new playlist and label it "Lucas' Musical Education". I start scrolling through my library looking for songs that would be appropriate for someone who never got into music. Without knowing what genre he might prefer, I start adding everything. A little rock, alternative, a few rap and hip-hop songs, even some country. I see a text message pop up on the top of my screen from Mark and it's in all caps. I roll my eyes and decide it's time to click on them. There are seventeen unread messages after all. I reach for my cocoa butter lip balm on the table and smooth it over my lips. I probably have a stick of it in every room in the house. Some people might call me obsessed. What can I say? I don't like chapped lips. And I don't like lipstick. My mother always said smooth lips were a must and I agree. I begin reading through his messages.

Mark: Dani. I'm sorry, okay? I think we can work this out. Please respond.

Mark: Dani, come on, this is ridiculous.

Mark: Dani!

I roll my eyes as they start to change.

Mark: Fucking answer me, bitch!

Mark: No one says no to me!

Mark: You're just a bottom of the barrel fuck toy anyway. I'm done with you!

Mark: BYE BITCH

Well, at least he's done. At least he "ended" it. Men like Mark just need the last word, just need to feel like they're still in control of a situation that isn't even a situation anymore. No use arguing with him. I'll let him have his last word and move on with my life. Good riddance and all that.

I check the clock and I still have some time before I need to get ready for work, so I grab my purse and head for the door. I make my way across the street and down the block to the little pharmacy. It's not a Walgreens or any big name. The name of the place is Hank's, and it's a pharmacy, hardware store, and grocery store all in one. It was one of those businesses that didn't take the hint when everything started changing. Despite Hank's slightly higher prices, the owner had loyal patrons that kept him going.

I walk down the aisles collecting a few things I need to

mail. The high school student behind the counter rings up my socks, lip balm, a pack of gum, a box of envelopes, and two twenty-five-dollar phone cards and I pay cash. I have cash in abundance usually. With the accumulation of tips each night, it goes in my pocket and my small paychecks go into my checking account. But I use cash to buy and pay for just about everything. Quinn calls me old school for this but I don't mind. I always know how much I have unlike most people who just watch their money disappear from an app on their phone and scratch their heads.

I get back up to my apartment after making the short walk back and Robert is waiting at my door.

"Did you get it?" he asks.

"Of course. What did you think, that I'd forget?" I pull out the pack of Juicy Fruit and rip it open. I pull out a piece and rip it in half.

We both open our ends and stick it in our mouths at the same time. Robert smiles and I smile. This is something we do together for a few reasons. Robert has dentures so he can only handle half a piece at a time. Plus, it's something he did with his late wife and he does it when he misses her. He does it to honor her. I'm happy to be a part of it.

Robert looks into my eyes and all I see is a grateful man, happy to have a friend to help him with this. Sometimes I go shopping for Robert because it's hard for him. And any time I go over to Hank's, I always pick us up some Juicy Fruit, his wife's favorite. He doesn't like the way it's changed but he eats it anyway. He pats me on the shoulder without saying a word and shimmies past me to the stairs to make his way back down to his apartment.

I walk into my apartment and sit the rest of the items on

the counter. I walk to the pantry and grab one of the flat boxes in there and begin making it and taping it. I feel my phone buzz in my back pocket and pull it out.

Quinn: Do you think you could do me a favor? Pretty please?!

This isn't good. Anytime Quinn asks for a favor, you can bank on it being something you absolutely do not want to do.

Me: That depends.

Quinn: Will you pretty please switch me and go into work at six and let me come in at eight??

I grimace and check the time. That's in twenty minutes!

Me: OMG could you have waited any later to ask me??

Quinn: I know, I know, but I'm on this date and he's so cute and it's going so great!

I sigh. Well, the girl hadn't been on a successful first date in six months so this does put me in a friendship dilemma. I want to be a good friend. I also don't want to go in at six though.

Me: Fine. You owe me!

I drop the box and run to my bedroom to get ready, cursing Quinn under my breath. Luckily, my clothes were laid out and decided upon. Otherwise, I'd be fucked. I throw on my shorts, bra, and shirt and slip on my boots. I run into my bathroom and brush my teeth first. I twist my hair back on one side with a bobby pin and fluff it up all over to try to give it some life. My hair has always been a point of contention. It's rather dull and flat most of the time. I pull out my make-up bag and check my phone. I need to be downstairs in nine minutes. I use some powder, a little peachy blush, and some mascara. As always, I finish with cocoa butter lip balm. I step back and take a look in my full-length mirror. It's not my best look but not my worst either. It's certainly a little less impressive than what I was going for but maybe that's in my head. I grab my keys and wallet, shove my phone in my back pocket, and make my way downstairs in a hurry.

I walk in one minute past when I was supposed to be here and Calvin looks up at me from his spot in the back corner. He eyes me for a second and checks his watch. He holds his watch up at me and taps it and I know it means he knows I'm late. I was hoping since this wasn't my original shift he might not know but it's clear Quinn had alerted him of the change, which is just another reason to curse her under my breath. I make my way over to the bar and tie my apron in place. I survey the room a bit, noticing it's not too busy just yet. Though, I had a feeling this would be a long night.

8

DANI

I'M NINE YEARS OLD. MY MOTHER HAS PUT ME IN THE closet again and I know enough to know my mother doesn't have a normal job like other parents. She doesn't have to leave for work. She's in the house all the time. Sure, our house is nice. I mean, I guess. It's not the biggest house, or the fanciest, but we have okay furniture and I have my own room and my bed is almost brand new. My mom doesn't even smoke inside like some people I know.

People come in and out a lot, though. Men, mostly. I wish they didn't. I know they're having sex. I don't know exactly what happens during sex but I know that's what's happening. They leave money with her and she tells me they're just massage clients, but something doesn't seem right about it. I nod at her simple explanations.

"What do you want for dinner, princess?" she asks me one night after all her clients are gone for the day.

"I don't know," I say, a little sadness in my voice.

"What's wrong?" she asks.

"Nothing," I insist. I always say nothing every time she asks. She knows I'll say it before she asks, I'm sure.

She looks at me and tilts her head. "Oh my princess, you're getting so big. Soon you'll be a woman," she says.

"I don't want to be a woman," I say. The thought frightens me. There's too much that happens, too much to deal with. What if becoming a woman means I have to have sex too?

"But you'll love it, darling. You can wear pretty dresses and high heels and make up. Don't you want to?" she asks.

"Mother?" I ask, because this feels like a mother moment rather than mom.

"Yes?"

"When I become a woman, will I have to have sex too?" I ask.

"No, my love. Never. You can be anything you want to be when you become a woman. Do you hear me? Anything at all. Don't ever let anyone tell you that you have to be a certain thing. You can even be more than one thing if you want. Do you understand?"

"Yes," I say.

A moment of silence falls over us and she moves across the length of the room to me. She pulls my face up by the chin to look me in the eyes. She smiles down at me and tucks a loose strand of hair behind my ear and runs her finger across my cheek. Finally, she leans in and hugs me tightly.

"Now. Enough of that. How about a nice, big stack of pancakes?" she asks me.

"Pancakes? For dinner?" I ask, excitement in my voice.

"Of course, why not? There's no law against it," she says, smiling big at me.

"My favorite!" I say.

"I know, my princess, I know," she says.

She starts pulling things from the kitchen cabinets to make the pancakes while I watch from one of the stools at the bar. I know she's doing this just for me, to cheer me up. Even at nine, I can tell I'm being bribed in a way. Distracted.

My mother always made things up to me. She was good at it. Apologizing without saying the words. She had a gift for it, a real talent.

I ate my pancakes that night. She sat across from me, watching intently, smiling. She made funny faces and tried to steal some bites of my pancakes. Most of the time I let her. She never made her own pancakes. Not even once that I can remember. She said they would give her cellulite, whatever that meant. Probably something I would have to worry about when I became a woman.

She took me by the hand and led me to my room. She laid me down and tucked me in tightly like a burrito. And then she sang. She always sang to me at bedtime. Some songs I recognized and some I didn't but I loved the sound of her voice so I didn't care what she sang. I drifted off, her face the last thing I saw before black.

I woke up some time in the middle of the night in a panic. I heard the noises, the night-time clients. There weren't many and they weren't all the time but somehow they were worse. They were louder. Sometimes I heard things break in the other room. Sometimes I heard their loud voices through the walls, their laughing. Sometimes I could hear my mother asking them to be quiet. I cupped my hands over my ears.

I could not escape it. I would never escape it.

9

LUCAS

I check the time on my phone for what must be the seventeenth time in the last thirty minutes. I am trying to wait patiently to go see Dani. I don't want to seem too eager so I will wait until an hour after her shift starts to show up. I figure that's a good plan. The only problem is, that's still an hour from now and I already want to go.

I feel my phone buzz in my pocket and pull it out.

Elliott: Hey, you wanna meet up?

God, this is so typical of him. No regard for anyone else, no explanation for standing me up or ghosting me for the past couple of days. Nothing. Just a stupid, impersonal invite like we hadn't spent the last eight years estranged. I write him back.

Me: Can't sorry, have plans

Elliott: Cool

And that's that. It would be another week or so before either of us say anything to each other. Even though he owes me eight years' worth of apologies. Even though he should be trying to make it up to me, make it better between us. Considering it was his fault. Whatever. I'll never get what I deserve. Some truth, some explanation.

I check my watch again and fourteen whole minutes had gone by. *Christ.* This is excruciating. Maybe I should go ahead and leave. I'll just take my time getting there. Maybe I'll stop off and get her something. *No wait, that's probably too soon.* I mean she doesn't exactly need a drink or food. She has both readily available. Flowers? *God no, how terrible would that be?* Somehow she didn't strike me as the type that wanted flowers.

Fuck it. I stand up and grab my wallet and keys. So what if I show up earlier? It wouldn't be a big deal. Maybe it would even make her happy. I don't know why I'm putting some much thought into this. It's not even that big of a deal. *Pull it together, man.*

I walk downstairs and head over to the bar where Dani works. I think about taking my car but I think it would be better to walk. That way when she gets off we can walk together. I happen to think this is a better idea than driving together somewhere. It provides a lot more opportunity to look at her and I am in favor of that. *I wonder what she's wearing tonight.*

I shake the thoughts from my head and keep walking. I feel my phone buzz again and look down at it long enough to see Chelsea's name pop up. *No way. Not again. I thought that was all done with. What the hell is her deal?* I shove my phone back in my pocket and ignore it. It's the best thing to do at this point. She would have to just let go on her own. I feel another buzz and don't even bother pulling it out.

Several minutes later, I'm standing outside Dani's work. Given everything, I'm nervous about going in. I don't even know why. I just feel vulnerable around her. Exposed. It's unsettling and I like it but it also frightens me. I have to keep a tight grip on this one. I have to play it cool and calm. I have to get into character.

I open the door to the bar and step inside. The place is a little busy but I would expect nothing less. I make my way through the crowd to an open bar stool and take a seat. I don't search for her until I am settled. I look one way and then the other. There she is at the far end. She's popping the caps off beer bottles and sitting them down in front of some guys who clearly recognize just how attractive she is. She smiles her customer service smile while I make it a point to check her out from the neck down. I'm not disappointed. She could probably wear a potato sack and be gorgeous. I think she knows it too but not in a bad way.

"Can I get something for you, hun?" a voice asks, catching my attention from my other side.

I swing around to see another woman behind the bar. She seems very neat and proper and while I'm sure she would do a fantastic job, I only want one woman to serve me my drinks tonight. "Actually, I was waiting on Dani," I say.

The woman's eyes light up. "Oh! I'll get her for you!" she says.

I watch her walk down to Dani and tap her on the shoulder. She leans in and whispers to her and Dani looks up in my direction and the other woman points. Then Dani smiles her real smile. The one that makes the dimple on her left cheek show up. Her customer service smile doesn't do that.

I watch the other woman stay behind to serve the patrons at that end while Dani makes her way to me.

"Hey stranger," she says.

"Hey you," I say.

"So you didn't trust Quinn with your Heinekens?" she asks.

"I'm sure she would have done a fine job but I just couldn't bring myself to cheat on you. You're the only one who should be handling my beer," I say.

She laughs and turns to grab me one from the cooler. She pops the top off and sits it in front of me. "Can I get you anything else? We have a pretty good bacon cheeseburger and amazing mozzarella sticks."

"Well what kind of person can say no to either of those things? Which means I'll have both," I say.

"Are you a bit starved?" she asks.

"Maybe. It's very possible. I'm a growing boy," I say.

"Coming right up," she says, and walks down to enter the order.

I like watching her walk away almost as much as I like her laugh. I start to look around at the other people at the bar so as not to just stare at her like a creep. This place has a relaxed atmosphere. The crowd is calm but lively, fun. I feel my phone buzz in my pocket.

Chelsea: It doesn't have to be like this.

Chelsea: Won't you at least think about it?

Chelsea: Lucas please…

I can't do this with her again. I pull her contact up and block her number. It's better this way. She needs to let go.

I turn back to my beer and take a few sips and watch Dani work. She smiles at the patrons and pats their arms. All very customer service appropriate. They seem to really respond to her. I wonder how long she's been working here and tell myself to ask later.

She grabs food from the side and skips my way. "Here you go, hungry man," she says, smiling and sitting my plates down in front of me.

I rub my hands together and lick my lips to match her playfulness. "Stand back, Dani, this may impress you," I say, and smirk at her.

She nods her head. "I think we have two very different ideas of what's impressive in the opposite sex." She giggles.

She's probably right. I don't know why men pride themselves on how gluttonous they can be. And I don't know why we think others should be impressed by it. Still, I'm going to tackle this and tackle it good.

I make easy work of my food while she serves her other patrons. She looks my way and I lean back to rub my belly and gesture at the empty plates.

She comes to collect them. "Come on, it's time for my last break," she says.

I follow her out to the alley behind the bar where she leans against the brick building and sighs. I watch her shoulders slump.

"Rough night?" I ask.

"Not particularly. It's all the same. Sometimes I just feel

like I've been holding my breath all night and when I get out here, I can finally exhale," she says.

I understand and nod. "It's so quiet out here on this side. Hard to believe the hustle going on inside and on the other side of this building."

"Right? I never understood it either, but I look down this alley and there's hardly ever anything going on, almost no movement. I could swear I was somewhere else entirely," she says.

I take a look down the narrow alley road. A few trash cans and back doors to places but no one is parked back here. It really is quite ominous. "So you're not scared being back here all alone when you don't have the likes of me to come with you?" I ask.

"The likes of you? What are you, the defender of women who are all alone?" she asks.

"Well sometimes. Sometimes I'm sure they don't need me," I say.

"I fall into that second category, if we are categorizing," she says.

"I don't know, I don't really like categorizing. I prefer to let people be who they are and try not to compare them to others," I say.

"Same," she says. "Oh hey, I have something for you. I was going to wait until later to give it to you, but I think maybe you should do it while I finish up in there. Stay out here where it's nice and quiet and give it a real effort, okay?"

"Um, okay? What is it?" I ask, apprehensively.

She pulls her phone out and asks me for my number.

I give it to her and take my phone out.

"Okay, it's sent. Here, you will need these," she says, reaching into her pocket and handing me a set of earbuds.

I eye them quizzically and take them from her. My fingertips graze the skin on the back of her hand and I hear her inhale. *I wasn't expecting that either.*

"What's going on here?" I ask with a furrowed brow.

"I just can't accept that you don't like music. I've compiled a playlist of some really great stuff from a bunch of genres and I want you to listen and see what speaks to you. Just sit down on this stoop and I'll be back," she says, opening the door to step back into the bar.

I nod in agreement and decide to take her assignment seriously. I do just what she asked me to do and park myself on the stairs to unroll the earbuds. I plug them into my phone and bring up her message. She sent me the link to the playlist. I push play and concentrate. The first song is definitely a country song, I think. He's got a smoky voice. The lyrics are good. This song is moody and sad. I take a look at the screen. "Hurt" by Johnny Cash. This isn't so bad.

The next song comes on. It's completely different from the first. A woman's sultry voice is in my ears. It's raspy and beautiful and she sounds like she could run the world if she wanted. The beat is infectious. I look at the screen to see "You Should See Me in a Crown" by Billie Eillish. I've heard of Cash but never this woman. I like her a lot. I could listen to more of her. The next song comes on. It's folksy, slow, and haunting. Gregory Alan Isokov singing "If I Go, I'm Goin'". It's actually really lovely.

I listen to each song exactly as she's ordered them in her list. I think about how she sat and did this for me. Such a simple but meaningful gesture. I think about what must have made her pick these songs. Why these songs? Before I realize, it's ten songs later and I'm smiling and she's tapping me on the shoulder. I whirl around and she's smiling too. *Wow.*

"So, what do you think?" she asks.

"Wow," is all I can manage.

"Does that mean you found something you like?" she asks, her face brightening at the possibility.

"Yeah, a few actually. Most of them, if I'm being honest," I tell her.

She hops up and down on her toes and she's pleased with herself. "Ready to go?"

"Where are we going?" I ask.

"Not far, if it's okay with you."

I don't understand what she means but I follow her as she steps out onto the sidewalk in front of the bar and turns right. She walks quietly until she stops in front of a red door not far from the bar and I look around in confusion.

"Um, this is my place. I know we can't go to yours and I thought maybe we could take a walk or something but honestly, I've been on my feet all night and I'd like to just be able to sit comfortably and talk. If that's okay with you?" she says.

I get the impression she doesn't usually open her own place up to people. She seems hesitant and even a little vulnerable. I have so many questions for her.

"I think that would be really great," I say, tucking my hands into my front pockets.

She smiles and takes her keys out.

Do not have sex with her. Do not have sex with her. Not yet. Don't do it. I will try really hard to be good, to be gentlemanly. I will try really hard to be more than I am.

MARK

THAT'S WHERE THE BITCH LIVES?! FUCKING TWO DOORS over? What the fuck?

I watch intently from a shadowed area across the road. I can only tell it's her from her blonde hair until I look down. I'd know that ass anywhere. *Who the fuck is that with her?* I can barely see the guy and his back is toward me almost the entire time. I can't see shit from here. *Since when does a bitch blow me off and then take some dude home? She never even took me to her place. She said it was a rule. What the hell?*

I watch them walk up the stairs and pause as she opens the door. They go in and I wait, looking at the windows. A few seconds later, the lights in a third-floor apartment come on and I know that one is hers.

She'll pay for this. I don't get like this. She'll pay for sacking me in the groin. I iced my junk for half an hour before I could move. Fucking bitch. I sit there, staring at the lights on in the window. They're probably fucking by now. That's all she's good for anyway. I take a shot from my flask and stick it back in my pocket.

I have to wait for a better time. I can't do anything now. I had it all planned out and this asshole ruined it. But the time will come. I'll get her alone again. I can be a patient man.

I'll get her.

I flip the light on in the living room and immediately start taking my shoes off. My feet are killing me. I turn back to the door and Lucas is still standing right next to it.

"Come in, silly. Make yourself comfortable," I say.

He relaxes his shoulders a bit and starts looking around. "This is a really nice place."

"Why thank you, I appreciate that," I say. "I'm just going to go change really quick. I smell like beer and grease." I walk back through the short hallway to my bedroom while he probably begins snooping in the living room. Let's face it, that's what we do when we are in someone's place for the first time. Although, I don't usually let people in here. He doesn't seem like the crazy type though, so I hope I won't regret it later.

I peel out of my work clothes and grab some leggings and a slouchy off-the-shoulder t-shirt. This is cute enough and comfortable enough. I walk back out into the living room and Lucas is standing in front of my bookshelf.

"Find anything good?" I ask.

"Who's this?" he asks, pointing at the single framed photo on the whole shelf, which means I don't even have to look to answer.

"My mother," I say.

"She's very beautiful," he says.

"Yes, she was."

"Oh, I'm sorry," he replies.

"Would you like some wine or something?" I ask, making a very blatant attempt to change the subject.

I think he senses my reluctance to talk about her as he nods. He walks over to the couch and sits down. I take two glasses from the cabinet and grab the open bottle of wine from the counter and head into the living room to join him.

"So how long have you worked downstairs?" Lucas asks.

"Just a couple of years," I say. "I worked at a place across town before that and it was a pain in the ass so downstairs is a lot more convenient."

"Commuting can be a bitch," he says.

"Well, I don't have a car, so it was a little worse than that," I say.

"Why not?" he asks.

I pour two glasses of wine and sit the bottle back down. "I guess I just never needed one. I've always lived in the city. I live and work close. Everything I need is close. I don't like traffic. I prefer walking anyway. I guess I just don't see a point."

"So, do you have a license? Like have you ever driven?" he asks, his curiosity growing just like anyone else who's ever asked.

"Of course I do and of course I have." I hand him his glass and sit back with mine, crossing my legs in front of me and twisting my body toward him on the couch.

"Interesting," he says, sitting back and taking a sip from his glass.

"Most people do find it interesting, actually," I say. "Not that I understand." I take a second sip from my glass as it falls quiet.

"How long have you done this?" Lucas asks.

I know what he means. "I guess all my adult life. I didn't date in high school. A few too many personal issues at the time to deal with that," I say. "How long have *you* done this?"

"Pretty much the entire length of the marriage. So, eight years or so. I wasn't too pristine before that either. I guess I'm just restless. Maybe I wasn't meant to settle down," he says.

I take in what he says, the honesty of it. "Do you think you'll stop?" I ask.

"Maybe. I mean I hope so," he says.

"Why do you snap a rubber band on your wrist?" I ask.

"It's something to help with my anxiety and thoughts. Believe it or not, I have a lot of negative thoughts about myself. The rubber band is my way of trying to replace at least some of them with some other action. To keep control. I also tend to snap it when I'm nervous," he says.

I nod my head, understanding in this moment that perhaps Lucas is maybe a little more sensitive than first perceived. "What's your favorite color?" I ask.

"Do you have question Tourette's?" he asks.

"Maybe."

"I like green," he says. "You?"

"I like gray. Gray is my identity. I'm just a gray area," I say.

"I don't think you're gray, but I will take your word for it," he says.

"What color am I then?" I ask.

"I don't know yet. I'll tell you when I figure it out." He smiles.

We spend the next hour or so like this, exchanging both meaningful and meaningless questions and answers. It's nice to sit and talk with someone like this. I don't do a lot of it, especially with someone of the opposite sex. I keep those interactions either business or sexual in most cases.

"What was your childhood like?" he asks.

I don't really like this question. I don't want to answer it. But I don't want to lie either. "Um, it wasn't great. It wasn't terrible either. Just normal, I guess. What about yours?" I ask. That wasn't the entire truth, but no one wants to hear about foster care and a hooker mother.

"Well, my mother remarried after my biological father died and they had another son, my half-brother. It was okay, I guess. My mother was happy so I tried to be happy, but my stepdad wasn't a very nice man, at least not to me. My brother was a chip off the old block. We never really got along. My mother died a couple of years ago. And since then, I've been trying to smooth things over with my brother since he's my only family left really. Some drama went down between the two of us a long time ago and we really haven't spoken since," he says.

"What kind of drama?" I ask.

"The kind of drama you save to talk about on a third or fourth date," he says, grinning at me.

I smile back. He does make me smile a lot. He makes it easy. "Can I ask you one last question?" I ask.

"Of course," he says.

"Do you want to kiss me?" I ask.

"Of course," he says again.

I lean up to sit my glass down on the coffee table and tuck my hair behind my ear. I turn back to him, sitting up a bit. "What are you waiting for?" I ask.

He bites his bottom lip and his eyes run over my neck and jaw and mouth. I like the way he looks at me. He makes me uneasy. Not many have been able to do that.

He sits forward a bit and puts his own wine glass down. "I was waiting for permission," he says, his voice lower now, deliberate.

"You need me to say it?" I ask, my own breath getting heavy.

He leans in closer and I feel my heart starting to race. He

lifts his hand up and caresses my jaw. He runs the tip of his thumb over my bottom lip and I close my eyes.

"I don't need you to say it, but I want you to," he says, his words almost a whisper into my hair. I inhale sharply.

"Kiss me," I say, eyes still closed.

And then I feel his lips pressing against mine, mouth parted. I feel the tip of his tongue meet mine. His hand moves back into my hair as he pulls me into him, into this kiss that travels down my sternum, bolts through my stomach, and causes the center of me to quiver.

It might have lasted ten seconds or ten minutes, I'm not sure, but as he pulls back, I find myself lusting for more. I take a breath and open my eyes to find him gazing at me, lids heavy, but a wild look in his eyes that is unmistakable. He looks hungry again. Hungry for me. I'm sure I have the same look on my face.

"Damn," he says, exhaling, a smile spreading over his lips.

And I agree. *Damn.* I run my hand through my hair as if that somehow helps me gain my composure. "Agreed," is all I can manage.

Our eyes meet again and the next thing I know, I find myself crossing the short distance between us and throwing my leg over to the other side of him. I sit on his lap, straddling him and pushing him back into the couch with my body. He wraps his arms around my waist and rests his hands on my lower back. My mouth meets his again, open and wanting. I run my fingers over his chest and up his neck and into the hair at the nape of his neck. I nibble his lip and he breathes in, his hands moving to my hips, his thumbs pressing into my hip bones. I am in a haze, drunk off him.

I realize a few minutes in that we are actually making out like a couple of teenagers and I giggle and pull away.

"What so funny?" he asks, puzzled.

"We are making out like a couple of teenagers," I say, giggling again.

"Well, I was really enjoying it," he says.

"Oh, me too," I say, still straddling him, still close to him. Our hands are still all over each other and our eyes meet again. I wonder if he's wondering the same thing I am.

"What now?" he asks, and I know he is.

I knew we are both wondering if we should stop now or let this happen. In the past, there was no question I would already be sleeping with the guy. After all, that's what these types of things are all about. And this feels right, it feels good. But do I want this to be like the others? It feels different somehow. We talk so much. I don't normally do that.

I reach up and run my fingers over the scruff on his chin, staring at him for a few moments. "What do you want to do?" I ask, wanting to hear it.

"Do you need me to say it?" he asks, grinning, repeating the words I said earlier.

I return the favor. "I don't need you to say it, but I want to hear it."

"I want to make you feel good," he says.

I inhale and bite my lip, considering his words. "So, make

me feel good, Lucas," I say, whispering my words against his neck and nibbling.

I feel his hands beneath me, lifting me up from him. He stands up and wraps my legs around him. He kisses my mouth and begins walking toward my bedroom.

"Are you sure?" he asks.

"Yes," I say, exhaling.

He pushes my door open with his foot and walks over to my bed, kissing me again before sitting me down on the edge. He looks down at me and runs his thumb over my lips again. I am aching now, and I think he knows. He gently pulls my top off over my head and it drops from his hands to the floor. I reach for him, but he stops my hands and kisses the palms of them and then puts them on either side of me. His eyes are tracing over my bare shoulders. I feel his fingers trace over my bra until he reaches the clasp and makes easy work of it. My arms let it fall and I drop it to the floor.

"Beautiful," he says, as his eyes travel over all my exposed skin. He traces his fingers from my lips down my throat and across my collarbone.

I feel goosebumps raise on my bare skin and then I feel his fingers traveling down my left breast. His two fingers trace around my nipple and I let out a moan as I raise my chin up to look at him. His mouth is parted, his breathing is jagged, and I am waiting for his next move.

His hands gently push me back onto the bed and I willingly lie down, my legs still hanging over the side. He hooks his fingers into the top of my pants on both sides and begins to pull them down. I lift up a little to let him pull them all the way off. I am completely naked now, but he hasn't taken any of his own clothes off. His eyes once again trace over all of me but I don't feel nervous. His hands graze the tops of my thighs as he kneels. He parts my legs and his hands trace up the inside of my legs.

My breathing quickens and I feel him kiss the inside of my knee. I moan again. He kisses me again a few inches higher and a few inches higher still. I feel him pause where my leg creases. I close my eyes and try to still my breathing but before I can his mouth takes me. My back arches and my hands find his hair again. His face pushes into me and I moan louder. *This is ecstasy. This is heaven.* I can't stop what's happening. I feel my body responding. I feel it giving in. Before I know it, I'm shuddering and moaning and finally catching my breath.

He pulls back, licking his lips and caressing my thighs. He stands and watches as what he's done to me rolls over my body again. After a few more seconds I can make eye contact with him. I'm smiling and he's smiling and finally pulling his shirt off.

Damn. He's beautiful. His arms and chest are flexing and defined. His smooth abdomen makes me wonder if he was a swimmer again. He starts to unbutton his pants and I can feel my excitement building again. He lets them fall and I am not disappointed. I want him. He climbs onto the bed and hovers over me as we both reposition ourselves all the way on the bed. He leans down and kisses my lips. My hands travel down his sides and I feel him inhale against my mouth.

He stops and looks at me. *This is it.* I don't know if he's just double checking with me or pausing for effect, but I pull him down against me to reassure him. And then he's inside me and I finally exhale again as his warmth travels over me. *God. This is amazing.* Our bodies are in rhythm now and we're kissing and moaning, and everything is so perfect and intense and passionate. *It's never been like this. I've never felt this.*

I push away the things I'm feeling and concentrate on the here, the now. Everything is building again, for both of us this time.

"Are you ready?" he whispers to me.

"Yes," I say. "I'm ready, I'm ready." I say.

He wraps his arms around me, and we release together. Our bodies are shaking, and he collapses into me. I let my body go limp under him and we lie there, catching and steadying our breaths. He rolls over next to me and begins running his hands through my hair. I begin to laugh, the sort of deep breathy laugh you have as if to say, "Damn, that was good", and he joins me. I look over at him.

"So, was that good for you or?" he asks.

"Um, very," I say. "You?"

"Oh yes, I think that will do just fine," he says.

We both retreat into silence, basking in the aftershock of it, of us.

After a little while, he sits up and looks around.

"You have a nice bedroom," he says.

I laugh. "Thanks. I wanted it to be a relaxing space." I know neither of us know what to say. I want to ask him to stay the night, but I know he can't. He has a life to get back to. "I guess you should probably go, huh?" I ask, saying it before he has the chance.

He looks down at his left hand and nods without saying a word. He stands up and starts putting his clothes on.

Maybe I shouldn't have said that. Fuck.

I get up and start putting my clothes on too. When we finish, he takes me by my hand, and we walk to the front door together like that. He turns and places his hands on either side of my face. He leans down and kisses me softly on the lips. I hug his waist and rub my hands over his shoulder blades. I can hear "Do You Mind?" by The XX in my head. I don't want him to go and that's not like me.

He pulls back from me and kisses my forehead. I smile.

"I'll text you when I get home, okay?" he says.

"Okay," I say.

He opens the door and walks backwards out.

I close and lock it after he disappears down the stairs. I stand there, leaning against my door and running my fingers over my lips. Tonight is the first time I feel disappointed that someone left. I don't know how to feel about that. I replay the events of the night in my mind and realize I enjoyed talking with him just as much as I enjoyed the sex which didn't happen very often. In fact, I can't remember it ever happening. Perhaps because I never gave it a chance to happen.

I make my way back to my bedroom, turning lights off as I go. Flipping the bedroom light on briefly, I smile and turn it back off. My body wants me to go to sleep but I need to wait for Lucas to text me so I apply some lip balm and try to straighten up my bed. I flip on the television and pull my weighted blanket up over me and nestle into the center of the bed. Investing in a weighted blanket to calm me down at night was a sound choice and when you don't share the bed with anyone you can afford to be selfish with the bedding. I am flipping through the channels when I hear my phone buzz.

Lucas: I'm home but I'm not happy about it.

Me: Why is that?

Lucas: I liked where I was half an hour ago better.

Me: Well, maybe you can stay next time?

Lucas: When is next time?

Me: I guess that's really up to you.

Lucas: I'll see what I can do.

Me: Good ;)

Lucas: Get some sleep, nerd.

Me: Oh, I plan to. I'm tired. Someone really wore me out earlier.

Lucas: Sounds like a lucky man.

Me: Now who's the nerd?

Me: Goodnight you.

Lucas: Goodnight.

I plug my phone in on my bedside table and snuggle back into my nest. I toss and turn a few times, repositioning myself over and over again but I can't seem to get comfortable. I close my eyes and try to find some calm space in my mind. I'm still replaying the events of the night and it hits me.

I don't want to be going to sleep alone tonight. *Damn.*

12

LUCAS

I wake up the next morning and for the first time in a long time, I am disappointed to be in my own bed. I know she asked me to leave because she thought I probably needed to. It felt like she wanted me to stay. I wanted to stay. I sort of hate myself for leaving. *Wow, this is a terrible way to wake up.*

I roll over and look at my phone and I have no messages, so I roll back over and shut my eyes. I consider going back to sleep for a little while, but my thoughts take over again. *I wanted to stay with Dani. I never want to stay. What the hell? I don't know if that's good or bad but I'm going to try to push it aside for now. Fuck, I have to work today.*

I get up and head for the bathroom to shower. *Should I text her? No, Lucas, no. Don't do it. Not yet.* I turn on the water and let the temperature regulate as I pull my clothes off and step in, letting the water hit me square in the face for several seconds. I wash up and get out without letting my thoughts wander too far. *Should I text her now? No, Jesus, shut up.* I get dressed and grab my keys and phone and start down the stairs. I open my car door and slide behind the wheel. *Okay, I'm texting her now. This is stupid.*

Me: Good morning you. Off to work and thinking of you.

I stare at the text before sending. *Should I send that? Is that too mushy? What the hell is going on with me?* I backspace a bit and revise.

Me: Good morning you. Off to work and thinking about last night.

Okay, yeah, maybe that's better. Less…something. I stare at the screen for a full minute seeing if she responds but nothing. I put my phone down and pull into the road. I can't let her distract me this much. I need to focus on literally anything else. I start thinking about the workload today and hear my phone buzz. *Shit, okay, I'll just look when I stop.*

I pull into the parking lot at work and pick up my phone.

Dani: Good morning you. What was your favorite part of last night?

I consider the question for a moment and formulate a response.

Me: That first kiss is still lingering.

Me: Then again, tasting you is still very much on my mind.

I smile at the thought. I have to keep this casual. We both know what this is, what this is supposed to be.

Dani: I enjoyed that part too.

Dani: Have a good day at work. You might not be able to reach me later, but I'll message you back when I can.

Me: All right, have a good day.

Dani: I'll try.

I wonder what would keep her from being able to text but then realize it's none of my business and put it out of my mind. If she wanted me to know she would have told me. I get out of my car and walk into work completely unmotivated. Today is going to be a long day.

I should probably text Elliott and see if today is good for him. If Dani isn't going to be available, I might as well. I smile involuntarily just at the thought of her name and curse under my breath. I'm such a dumb fuck.

I try to reason with myself. It's new and that makes it exciting, that's all. No big deal. It's always like this in the beginning. Except it's not. And I know it. Sure, I've had my fair share of fun and good sex but all that? That connection while talking? That's not usually part of the package. I don't even usually entertain it. She's just really easy to talk to. Too easy maybe. I'm not usually one for pillow talk but with her, I look forward to it. So much for focusing on something else and not letting Dani overpower all your thoughts.

I get to my office and shut the door. I have some time before the morning meeting, so I use it to answer emails and return some messages. I check the clock fifteen minutes later and hate that it's only been fifteen minutes. I decide to text Elliott.

Me: I'm free this evening if you want to meet up?

I keep working while I wait for a response and surprisingly it comes pretty quickly.

Elliott: Can't tonight. But definitely can Wednesday?

Me: Okay, that works for me. You want to go to that place you sent before?

And I'm hoping he says yes so I can use it as a means to see Dani at the same time.

Elliott: No, let's grab dinner at this place close to my work. I'll send you the address later.

Me: Okay.

Elliott: Cool.

I go back to work and check the clock and it's only seven minutes later than it was and I snap my rubber band three times. I decide the only way I'm going to get through it is to really dig in and just deal with it.

I'm kidding myself. I know that. I spend my work day thinking of Dani and cursing the clock. I want to see her tonight but wonder if it's too much too soon. I wonder if she will wonder how I have so much availability. Perhaps it's not a good idea. I have to get a handle on this.

I snap my rubber band at my self-loathing thoughts and realize I may have made my life even more complicated than it was before, if that's even possible.

13

DANI

I AM ELEVEN YEARS OLD MAKING MYSELF TOAST IN THE kitchen. My mother has gone to the grocery store to pick up some things and I hear a knock on the door. I expect to open the door and find my mother with her hands too full to open it herself, but I don't.

"Is Charlotte here?" a man asks. His voice is rough and he's smoking a cigarette and his eyes make me uneasy. He's swaying back and forth and catches himself with his hand before hitting his face on the door jam.

"No, not right now," I answer.

"Well, where is she?" he asks, urgency and anger growing in his tone. His face is getting too close to mine and I pull mine back a little.

"She'll be back any moment, she's just gone to the store," I say.

"Well, I'm coming in to wait," he says, pushing at the door with one hand.

I try to hold the door in place, but my small body is no match.

The door gives way and he walks in, swaying some more. He looks around and back at me. "So, who are you?" he asks.

"I'm Danielle," I answer quickly.

"Are you her daughter?" he asks.

"Yes," I say, voice as small as my body.

"How old are you?" he asks, his eyes tracing up and down my frame. He tilts his head at me like he's looking for something specific.

"Eleven," I say. I back away toward the kitchen and put the counter between us. He watches me and tilts his head to the side again, studying the way I move.

"Have you gotten your period yet?" he asks.

My face starts to get hot at his question and I can feel my heart pounding hard in my chest. I don't want to answer his questions. I don't want him to be here. I want my mother. I shake my head at him.

"No? Really? Shouldn't be too long now. Then you'll be a woman. But if you ask me, I like it like that. The way it is now," he says.

And I don't understand his words. "The way what is now?" I ask him. I hear my toast pop up and I ignore it. I don't want to put my back to him.

"Your body. It's still a girl, still so innocent," he says.

He's walking toward me now and my hands start shaking. There's nowhere to run to get away from him. The doors in our house don't lock. He stands in front of me and his body towers over mine.

"I think I should go to my room while you wait for my mom. She'll be here any minute," I remind him.

My words don't seem to stop him, and he rubs my shoulder while he glares at me. He looks down the front of my shirt and taps the top button with his finger.

"Maybe I should help you," he says. His fingers begin to unbutton my shirt.

"No, please don't," I beg.

He's not listening to me. I reach up to push his hands away and I can smell beer on his breath, and this is all wrong and I'm trying not to panic. He pushes my hands away and grabs my wrist.

"Didn't your mother ever tell you that you should be polite to guests?" he asks.

There's no use trying to resist him. I can't wiggle free and I can't stop him. I keep my head down and I feel him pull my shirt off. I have a training bra covering my flat chest. I don't know what to do.

"Please stop," I say, my words nearly a whisper.

He bends down and buries his face into my neck and hair and inhales deeply. "I'm going to do whatever I want to you and you can't stop me. Don't worry, I'll pay. I always pay," he says.

I feel him press his tongue against my neck and licks up to my cheek. I close my eyes and feel like I might faint right there on the kitchen floor. I feel his hand on my back.

"What the fuck do you think you're doing?" I hear my mother's voice at the front door and open my eyes. She's standing there staring at me and this man and I freeze.

"Oh hey, Charlotte. I was just sampling the menu. I think I want this fresh meat here," he says, looking toward my mother.

"That's not going to happen. You should leave now," she says. Her voice is calm but stern.

He looks at her, confusion and defiance in his eyes. "I'll pay extra," he says.

"Fuck you," she says.

"Listen here, you whore, this is what I want, and this is what I'm going to get. It's not like there's anything you can do about it," he screams back at her.

"There's plenty I can do," she says. She sits the bags down and closes the door behind her. I watch as she walks to the bookshelf between the kitchen and living room.

"Oh what, you gonna call the cops? We both know you're not gonna do shit," he says.

Right then, my mother looks me in the eyes. "Everything is going to be all right, princess. Okay? I want you to go to your room and get in your castle, okay?" she says to me.

I nod and he lets go of my wrist.

"I'll see you in a minute," he says to me.

And I run from him. I close my bedroom door behind me and run into my closet. I close that door too and flick on my flashlight. I don't hear anything at first. It's quiet and all I can do is wait. After a few minutes, I hear their voices getting loud again but I can't make out what they're saying. I hear one thud, and then another. I hear a glass break and I jump. I reach for the closet knob and stop myself. I know the rule. Wait for her. Always wait for her.

I hear another glass shatter and then I hear him scream. I don't know what to do. My body won't move even when I urge it to. Fear has consumed me. I push myself far into the back corner of the closet and the noises continue. Then everything grows quiet and I wait. I hear sirens outside next and a few more crashes and then everything is silent again. I hear the front door bang open and more yelling. It's quiet again and I'm still waiting. This pattern of quiet and loud, quiet and loud has my nerves in shambles. I don't know how much time has gone by. I close my eyes and wait some more.

My bedroom door opens gently, and I hear footsteps approach the closet door. They pause and I hear someone touch the knob. I flick the flashlight off and try to make myself as small as I can. The door opens and I see it isn't my mother.

"Hi there," a woman's voice says. "Can you come out?"

I don't answer and I don't move. She puts her hand out for me, inviting me.

"Where's my mom?" I ask but she doesn't answer.

"We should get you out of here first, then we can talk okay?" the kind but strange voice says.

I hesitate but finally take her hand. She wraps a blanket around me and walks me out of my room.

Everything is broken. There's broken glass everywhere and

chairs are toppled over. A police officer tries to shield my face, but I see it.

There on the floor right in front of the bookshelf where my mother was standing is a mess of blood. Next to it, there's a body underneath a sheet. There's a knife across the floor, a trail of blood between the body and the blade. I begin to cry, and the officer takes me into her arms, and carries me out as fast as she can.

All I see now are the blue lights swirling. I hear people talking but their voices are in a fog around me. They put me in the back of a car and a lady sits with me. She is telling me that everything will be all right, but I know she's lying.

I know nothing will ever be the same.

14

—————

LUCAS

With Elliott and Dani both tied up today, I decide
to spend my evening reminiscing. It's not the greatest idea
I've ever had. After cleaning up the apartment and doing
some laundry, I settle down in front of the trunk in the
corner of my living room. I don't know what made me
decide to do this, or why. I just felt the need to dive into
some old things. Maybe it was the thought of seeing my
brother after so long. Maybe it was because of Dani,
though I couldn't say why.

I push the trunk open and take a look inside. Amid photo
albums and documents are a few children's toys and
trophies from my teenage years. I search to find what I'm
looking for. I pull two albums from the stack and sit back
on the floor. I wipe the dust from the top of the first one.
On the front is a picture of me and my mother. She made
this for me after she got sick. Every now and then I flip
through it and remember our time together. I open to the
middle and see a photo of me in front of a birthday cake
with her beside me. I turn the page and we are standing

beside a snowman in our backyard. I miss her. In many ways, she was the only family I really had. Regardless of what Elliott has done, he's the only family I have left and that's why I have to make it right.

I close the photo album of my mother and set it aside. I haven't held this other one in a really long time. The white satin front had yellowed and turned grungy over the years. I open it up and there she is. In the photo, I'm wearing a suit and she's wearing the long red dress I loved her in. Samantha and I were engaged and happy. Or so I thought. I stare at the picture, trying to detect any sign of how she truly felt in that moment. I can't see anything.

She wears her smile. Her arms are wrapped around me, head thrown back mid-laugh.

These were our engagement photos. She insisted on a professional session to mark the occasion. I didn't get it but agreed to make her happy.

I turn to the next photo.

The sun is setting in the skyline behind us, and our bodies are not much more than silhouettes. We are forehead to forehead, holding hands.

I remember each of these moments in my mind. I don't understand what I missed.

I flip to the back of the album and there's an envelope. I pick up the envelope and I can feel her engagement ring inside. The envelope is sealed, same as the day I got it. She wrote my name on the front. I've always assumed there was a letter inside, but I could never bring myself to open it.

I broke it off. That sounds less like the truth than I mean it.

What really happened is far more tragic, far more complicated. But I remember it like it was yesterday.

I came home early from work with flowers in hand. Samantha and I had gotten into a fight the night before and I wanted to apologize. I opened the front door and heard music upstairs. I sat my keys down in the kitchen and noticed a blazer neatly folded over the back of a chair. Slightly confused, I made my way upstairs and down the hall to our bedroom. I heard her scream out in laughter. My heart began to race. I reached the door and turned the knob slowly. I could hear another familiar voice on the other side. I remember gulping and trying to still myself.

When I opened the door, it took a few moments before they noticed me. Samantha was naked on top of a man, her back to me. I saw his legs, his arms wrapped up around her. She turned toward me, gasping. She read the shock on my face but said nothing. Just then, the man revealed his face to me, leaning over to look around her.

Elliott. Samantha and Elliott. My fiancé and my fucking brother. Fucking in my bed. In my shock, I didn't feel anger. I didn't feel anything really. I shut the door as I heard both of them yelling my name. My head in a fog, I walked down the stairs and out the door and got back into my car and drove away.

I never went back to that house. I had movers go get my stuff. I didn't return any calls or messages from either of them. She'd given this envelope to the movers and asked them to deliver it with my belongings. She didn't even have the guts to deliver it herself or talk to me in person. Sometimes I get curious enough to want to open it. Other times, I'm so angry I refuse to read it. I refuse to give her a voice in my head. I didn't want to read the excuses or reasons. I may never open it. Most days, I'm okay with that.

I flip the envelope over in my hands three times before wedging it back into the back of the album and shutting it. That was almost a decade ago and I needed all of that time to even muster the energy and strength to try to have Elliott in my life again. But as my only family, I had to bury the hatchet. I had to make it right. I promised my mother I would.

I put both albums back into the trunk and shut it. I rub my forehead with the palm of my hand and shut my eyes for a moment. Some days I'm not sure if this is the right thing to do. I check the clock and decide to try Dani again.

Me: Hey you.

I wait for a response, but it doesn't come immediately so I put my phone back down and take a shower. Maybe she will respond by the time I get out. She was a little MIA today, and she didn't add why and so I didn't ask. I was just hoping she didn't regret what happened between us.

I grab a towel and head for the bathroom when I hear my phone buzz. I decide to have my shower first before answering. I don't even walk back to check who it is. I know if it's Dani, I'll get too distracted. She causes me issues in the concentration department.

I start the water for my shower and climb in. I let my mind go for a second, closing my eyes and letting the water run over me. I try to rewind a bit. I think about the ring I keep on my finger. What if I didn't wear it? What if I met Dani without it? What if I could have taken her out on a normal date like a normal guy? I think about her looking at me, wanting to kiss me as a single man. Wanting to kiss me because she wanted me, not married me. I think about what would happen if I told her the truth now. I think about losing her. For the first time in a long time, I don't think I want that. Not yet.

15
___

DANI

EVERY fiRST MONDAY OF THE MONTH, I TAKE THE NUMBER
seventy-two bus forty-five minutes north to Shady Oaks.
That's where my mother is. That's where she will be
forever. I put my phone away after texting Lucas and enjoy
the rolling countryside as we exit the city. I have been on
this road so many times; I know the buildings, the barns,
and the signs before we get to them.

The bus stops short of the tall wrought iron fence and the
grandeur of the front gate is misleading. There is only
sadness inside. I walk through the gate with the others
who've come to visit their loved ones. Inside, we gather at
the chain link fence and remove our jackets and bags. We
take everything from our pockets and sit it in a plastic bin.
I walk through the metal detector the way I do each month
and get cleared on the other side by a woman wearing a
uniform and latex gloves.

I present my ID next and give my mother's name. They
wave me onward. I walk into the small enclosed courtyard

where small, round tables are scattered. I walk to the right corner farthest from me and sit down.

"Hello, my princess, my Dani," my mother says.

I smile at her as she cups my face in her left hand the way she does each time. "Hi, Mom," I say. "How are you?"

My mother sits back and looks down the front of her. She tries to straighten out her bright orange oversized shirt. A number is printed on the left breast—her identification number.

"Well, what can I say? Not much changes in here. It's all the same, all the time. But I did manage to get a few extra privileges this week," she says, attempting to fake genuine excitement.

"That's good, anything to pass the time, right?" I ask. My voice trails off at the end and we both know passing the time makes no difference. A life sentence is a life sentence. Whether it passes slowly or quickly, it doesn't change anything. Silence falls between us, the way it does at least once in a visit.

"So, my princess, your birthday is soon!" she says, changing the subject for both our sakes.

"It's no big deal," I say.

"Of course, it is! Your birth will always be the most important day for me, and certainly something to celebrate," she replies.

"It's just another year. I'll probably do what I always do. Nothing," I say.

She shakes her head at me and sighs. "Do me a favor, Danielle? Please?"

I know it's serious because that's the only time she ever calls me Danielle. "Anything," I say. And I mean it. I always mean it when she calls me Danielle.

"Celebrate your birthday. Really big. A party, with food and a cake and music and balloons and streamers and all that. Just this one time. Please?"

I press my lips together. I don't want to do that. I don't want to celebrate without her. "Okay, Mom. I will."

"And take a lot of pictures. Bring them to me. Okay?"

"I will," I say, shoulders slumping now. The thought of it makes me a little sick, but I'll do it for her.

"Good! That's settled. What else is new, my love?" she asks.

"Not much to report. Well, I mean I'm seeing this new guy," I say. My mother knows all about who I date and why. I would even go so far as to say she approves. She sort of even encourages it. She just gets me.

"And how's that going?" she asks.

"Really well so far, actually. I enjoy being around him, and he's funny," I say.

"Oh, my princess, be careful," she says abruptly.

"What do you mean?" I ask.

"You like him," she says.

"What? No, I mean I do, but no more or less than anyone else I've seen," I say, willing it to be true.

"Honey, I know you. And I know that look you have. It's dangerous. You probably shouldn't even see him again," she says.

I sit back, a little shocked, a little sure she's probably right. But I do what I want. "I'm seeing him again. He's fun," I say.

"Suit yourself," she says.

There's another moment of silence and she shifts the subject to what flavor of cake I will have.

We talk for another twenty minutes before it's time to go. We stand and hug the way we always do.

She tucks my hair behind my ears, smiling at me. "Take care of yourself out there," she says.

"Take care of yourself in here," I reply.

She nods. "Love you for life."

"Love you for always," I say.

I turn and walk back toward the gate. I don't look back. She asks me to never look back. I know it's because she's still standing there watching me until I am out of sight.

I make my way back to the bus, both happy to have seen her and sad this is all I will ever have of her. I miss her terribly between our visits. I stopped celebrating almost everything because I hate the idea of celebrating anything when she can't. The thought of planning a birthday party and celebrating it gives me more anxiety than I can handle. I have no idea how I'll pull this off. Plus, turning thirty isn't even something I'm looking forward to.

The night she came back from the store nineteen years ago changed everything for me. She did what any mother would do. She protected her child. She killed a man. And while in most cases, some jurors or judges could see this gesture for what it was, my mother was a prostitute. And the man she killed was someone a bit more important in the eyes of society. He was successful and wealthy and even though he was visiting such a person in the slums of the city, he was missed by too many other important people. And who missed my mother? Just me. No one important enough to save her from life in prison.

I board the bus and think back to foster care. They played ping pong with me. Here and there and back again. No real parents or role models. In the foster system, no one wants an eleven-year-old. Especially the daughter of a whore with no known father on record. On paper, I was trouble waiting to happen, a ticking time bomb. Perhaps they assumed I would follow in my mother's footsteps and start sleeping around. Maybe they thought the estranged father would come out of the woodwork. Whatever the reason, no one wanted me for more than a little while. It was harder as time went on. The older I got, the less interest I was given. When I turned eighteen, I aged out. They just let you go with no plan for the future and nothing to your name. You just sort of have to figure it out.

I've been on my own since I was eleven, even with the help of the system. It's always just been me looking out for me. It was better that way. If it couldn't be my mom, I didn't want anyone else anyway.

I look out the window of the bus again at the other side of the road and for a moment I forget everything. Forget the pain, the night everything changed, the ride here, where we are going. The fields are rolling by in a blur and for a moment I think maybe this bus can lift off the ground and never land.

I never wanted any of this.

I pull my phone back out and see a few messages.

Lucas: Oh, what's that song that played at your house when we kissed?

Quinn: Could you cover my shift on Wednesday? Pretty please? Xo

Lucas: Okay, you're busy, I know. I know. But are you free later?

I text Quinn back first and tell her I can cover for her. Then I turn my attention to Lucas.

Me: I should be back at my apartment in about an hour. Is that okay?

Lucas: Hey! Yes, perfect!

Me: Oh, and the song was "We Might Be Dead By Tomorrow" by Soko.

Lucas: Wow, intense title...

Me: Maybe a little lol

Lucas: Hungry? Want me to bring food over when I come?

Me: I'm famished.

Lucas: What would you like?

Me: Surprise me.

Lucas: Oh, woman. Prepare to be surprised.

Me: Deal :)

I take my headphones out and scroll through my playlists to find the song he asks about. I listen to it again as I make my way back into the city. Sometimes I miss this place and sometimes I hate this place. I can't decide what I'm feeling for it now.

I take the shortest route home from the bus depot and even

though I should be used to them, a siren going off and the whirling of blue lights in the background cause me to quicken my pace. I've never quite gotten the image of them that night out of my head. Sometimes you hold onto things, small things, insignificant details nearly irrelevant to the main event. But those small things are what stay fresh in your memory. They're the things that keep you up at night, the things that pull at the buried and long forgotten thoughts. If I'm not careful, the blue lights will drudge up every nuance of that night. I'll start to remember the way it smelled. I'll begin to see the blood stain pattern in my morning coffee when I pour in the creamer. I'll start to hear the breaking glass on busy nights at work.

I shake the thoughts and images from my mind as quickly as they tumble in, uninvited. *Focus on Lucas. Lucas can take your mind off it all.* I'll welcome any distraction at this point, but a good kisser is at the top of the preferred list.

I want to let him help me forget. I want to let him touch me, kiss it away. I want to let him wrap my body in his until it cannot feel the drunken stranger's hands that changed my life. I want him to replace all the pain with the pleasure I know he can give me. I want him to press his warm body against mine and drown me in anything other than what I'm feeling now.

I turn the corner to my apartment building and he's standing there with a bag in his hands waiting for me. I breathe for what seems like the first time in several minutes and I can feel my face light up. I take the sight of him in. I quicken my pace and I know my mother was right.

I might be in trouble.

16

LUCAS

I HEAR FOOTSTEPS BEHIND ME AND TURN TO LOOK OVER MY shoulder. Her blonde locks bouncing are unmistakable so I shift my body to watch her walk to me. I smile at her and she smiles back. She's just a few paces away now but I can see the warmth in her eyes, the excitement in her walk.

"Hey there," I say.

"Hey you, been waiting long?" she asks.

"Just a couple of minutes, no big deal." She's right in front of me now and I lean down to kiss her a proper hello.

"So, what are we having?" she asks, opening the door to let us in.

This is the part I'm most excited about. "Well, I hope you don't mind if I commandeer your kitchen?"

"No, not at all. Wait, does that mean you're cooking?" she asks, and I can hear the shock in her voice.

"Yes, ma'am, I am," I say.

"Wow. Okay," she says.

"What? Do I not look the type?" I ask, feigning offense.

"No, no it's not that. It's just, I've never actually had anyone cook for me. Not since I was a kid anyway," she says.

"Wait, what? How is that possible?" I ask.

"Well, I've never really been in an actual relationship, obviously. And the men I have seen, well I wouldn't exactly say showering me with attention was their objective," she says.

I read between the lines, knowing what she means. She means they were selfish, that they used her. She means she was nothing more than an object to them. I hated that for her. I snapped my rubber band so hard against my wrist I almost winced.

"Oh," I say.

"What?' she asks.

"Nothing, it's nothing. It's just, you deserved more from them, Dani. That's all," I say.

We make our way into her apartment and I sit the bags I have in my arms down on the counter. She sits her stuff down and turns to me.

"Thank you for saying that," she says.

And in the way she is thanking me, I realize no one's probably ever told her that either. I nod and smile. "Of course," I say.

She shifts on her feet a bit.

"Why don't you go get comfortable? You seem like you've had a long day," I say.

"That sounds like a good idea, but shouldn't I help you?" she asks.

"Absolutely not," I say. "I'm a big boy. I'm sure I can find what I need, and I brought everything else with me."

"Well, if you're not going to let me help, do you mind if I soak myself in a bath for a few minutes?" she asks.

"I think that's a great idea," I say. "I'll bring you a glass of wine."

She tilts her head at me and blinks a few times, seemingly surprised by my willingness to let her soothe herself. She turns toward the hall and I do what I love to do: watch her walk away. I start taking items out of the bags and organizing my little cooking space. Even though I don't cook for myself all that often, I actually do love cooking. I haven't cooked for anyone else in a long time, but I'm feeling confident. I hear her turn on the water and I search for a wine glass. After I find one in the cupboard, I poor a generous amount and make my way to the bathroom door and knock.

"Who is it?" she asks, teasing.

"A ruggedly handsome man looking to get you a little tipsy," I say.

I hear her laugh on the other side and I push the door open. I nearly drop the glass I'm holding at the sight of her. Her wavy tendrils are pulled up loosely on top of her head and she's leaning back against the tub, eyes closed, a relaxed smile on her face. She is beautiful, and she doesn't know it. Granted, the woman knows she's sexy. But she isn't aware of her raw and natural beauty. I walk over to the side of the tub and soap bubbles are wispy across the top of the water, concealing most of her body. This mystery excites me. She opens her eyes.

"This is for you, my dear," I say, leaning down to hand her the glass.

She takes it from me, our hands touching for a moment. "Thank you. I really need this," she says.

I wonder what today's been like for her, why she needs this soak. "Want to talk about it?" I ask.

She twists uncomfortably for a split second. "Not really. Why dwell on it when you can move on from it, you know?"

"I guess. I mean sometimes talking it out helps. Or just venting," I say. My smile widens.

"It's okay, really. I would rather just enjoy the evening with you," she says, sighing, swirling her fingers in the water, moving some of the bubbles around.

"Careful there, you're uncovering yourself," I say, not attempting to hide the fact that I am definitely checking her out now. I trace the lines of her body with my eyes. I trace the ink on her skin, suddenly filled with the urge to ask about them, why she has them, their significance.

"I meant to," she says, eyes narrowing on me.

I watch her hand make larger swirls. I watch more of her body appear. Suddenly, I find it very warm in here. I gulp, realizing my mouth is watering. I watch her trail her fingers down her thigh and my entire body reacts.

"If you want to eat, you should stop. I'll never be able to

leave if you keep this up," I say, running my fingers through my hair.

"You should go cook then. We're both going to need our strength," she says.

I audibly choke and she giggles. The grin that spreads across her lips is what makes strong men weak in the knees. I turn away before it's too late and reluctantly walk back to the kitchen to chop and cut and cook and think. She's unraveled me and she knows it. I turn my focus to the food. *Yes, the food.*

After a little while, I hear movement in her direction and the timing is just about perfect. I've put the finishing touches on our meal and now I just need to get it to the table. I'm sitting plates down in their spots and pouring more wine and positioning napkins when I hear her behind me. I can feel her watching me, but I don't turn around.

"Like what you see?" I ask.

"You do have a nice ass," she says. She's feisty tonight. She's open.

"Well, thank you. I don't believe that's a compliment I get often," I say. I turn around after I finish with the table and audibly choke again. My eyes start at her bare feet and travel up her legs. She's wearing the most delicate black panties I've ever seen. Her naked breasts are barely covered by a nearly sheer robe. She's taken her hair down; wild and messy locks brush back and forth on her shoulders. I am in awe of her again.

"Hi," she says.

"Hi," I manage.

"So, what did you make?" she asks.

"Are you going to sit across the table from me like that while I try to eat? Because that's cruel," I say.

"I thought you wanted me to be comfortable?" she asks, a hint of forced innocence in her voice.

I shake my head. "You're right, that's more important. Never mind my comfort," I reply, laughing nervously.

She walks the distance between us in just a few long strides and presses her body against mine. Her hands travel down my sides and I quiver. I lean down to breathe in the scent clinging to her neck. *Heaven.*

"Kiss me," she says, and I do exactly that.

I take her face into my hands and kiss her hard on her mouth. She rolls onto her toes and I lean in deeper. I pull back and kiss both her cheeks, then her eyelids, then her forehead.

"Still hungry?" I whisper.

"Definitely," she says.

I don't know if she's talking about the food or me but I lean back to pull her chair out so she can sit down. I walk around to the other side of the table and sit down in front of my plate. I stare across the table at her with an excitement, both about the food and what will happen after the food.

I watch her look down at her plate and see the surprise in her eyes. I made my favorite thing. It's not difficult or time consuming or even that fancy. But it's delicious.

"Well, I hope you like breakfast?" I ask.

"Are you kidding me? It's like my favorite thing," she says.

Her words echo my thoughts and I smile. "Me too," I say.

She looks up at me shocked. "Can you believe some people only eat breakfast in the morning? They're missing out," she says.

"I totally agree," I say. I watch her pick up her fork and start. I mirror her actions. "So, did your bath help you feel better at all?"

"Definitely. A good bath can help take the stress away," she says.

"I honestly don't remember the last time I took a bath," I say.

She looks up at me in shock. "Really? You're totally missing out," she says, putting a bite of eggs in her mouth.

"You know what I think it is?" I ask.

"What?"

"Well, I'm just so lonely in there all by myself. Maybe if I had someone to take one with me that would make me feel better about the whole experience," I say, shooting her my best sexy look.

She laughs and nods. "You know, maybe you're right. Maybe I can help with that sometime."

"Oh, I wish you would," I say.

She smiles at me and takes another bite. Our sexy banter goes on between bites and bits of conversation until we are sitting there in front of empty plates.

"That was delicious," she says.

"I'm glad you liked it," I reply, leaning back in my chair. It grows silent for a few moments and I watch a curiosity form behind her eyes.

"Come with me," she says, pushing back from her chair and holding out her hand.

I stand and fold my hand into hers.

She walks me to the bathroom and starts running more bath water.

"Didn't you just do this?" I ask.

"It's not for me," she says.

I tilt my head and watch her let the water run over the back of her hand for a moment. She plugs the drain and adds some salt stuff from a bottle, then some liquid stuff from another bottle. She turns to me and begins unbuttoning my shirt. She pushes it off my shoulders and it falls behind me. I try to reach for her, but she puts my hands back down beside me. I smile. I like this game.

She unbuttons my pants next, pulling them down at the same time as my briefs. Her eyes take me in, and I watch her breathing pick up. She turns from me and sticks her hand into the water to double check it.

"Okay," she says. "In you go."

I step over to the tub and put my foot in. The warmth from the water travels up my legs. I sit down into it completely and my body instantly slumps with relief.

"Lean back," she says, and I do as she tells me.

I'm in uncharted territory with bath time here. She takes a loofa and adds some liquid soap to it. She lathers it in until it begins to foam and then she crouches over me to rub it over my chest and arms and neck.

"This is better than I expected," I say. I close my eyes and let her pamper me.

"Okay, lean up now so I can get your back," she says. She repeats the soft, swirling motions over my back and up my neck and then rinses it away and pushes me back down into place. She rinses off the front of me and puts the loofa back on the side of the tub. She grabs a stool from behind her and sits beside me. "I'm glad you like it," she says, watching me fall into complete relaxation. "Hopefully it's helping melt away any stresses from your day."

"Oh, it is. Definitely," I say.

"You know what? I don't even know what you do for work. How has that not come up?" she asks.

I search my few memories and realize we never talked about it. "Well, it's nothing fancy, really. I'm a buyer for a construction company. I source raw materials and get deals and arrange shipments. It's all very boring but it pays the bills," I say.

"That doesn't seem boring," she says.

"You don't have to be nice," I say.

"Oh, I'm not," she says, shooting me that look she does. Brooding, heavy eyes. Lips parted.

This is the look that drives me wild. "You know, this bath is missing one thing," I say.

She looks around the tub, confused. "What?"

"You," I say.

She smiles at me. "You're smooth." She folds her arms over her chest.

I make a pouty face and push my bottom lip out. "Please?"

Without a word, she stands up and drops her robe. She steps in, one foot on each side of me and sits down, straddling me. "Like this?" she asks.

"I think you forgot to take something off," I say, looping my thumb into her panty line and tugging a bit.

"Oh no, those stay. I don't want you getting any ideas," she says, grinning at me.

"So, I'm just supposed to sit here and have a conversation with you with your breasts right in my face, and not want you?" I ask.

"Basically," she says.

I wrap my hand into her hair and pull her face down to mine. "Well, that's just evil," I say. I press my lips to hers, tasting the sweetness of her mouth. I press my tongue to hers and it sends a wave of adrenaline over me.

She pushes her fingers through my hair and pulls me into her. My hands travel down her back and cup her ass. I'm hard against her and she grinds down into me, letting me know she feels it too. She pulls her lips from mine.

"I want you, Lucas," she whispers into my ear.

And it's all I need to come completely unhinged. I hold her in place and sit up, letting her get up from my lap. I stand in the bathtub and pull her against me for another kiss. I step out and turn to grab her. I wrap her legs around me and take her into her bedroom.

"Your bed is going to get wet," I say, just before I throw her down on it. I climb on top of her gently, leaning down to kiss the small soft space between her tits. I kiss her collarbone and hear her moan. I kiss her neck and chin and make my way to her mouth. I part her lips with my tongue. I reach down with my hand and trail my fingers over her belly button and into her panties. I touch her and feel her body arch in response. She kisses me deeper and I tease her more. Her fingers grip the sheets and I can see she's close. I pull away and she moans again.

"Tease," she says.

I kiss the tip of her nose. "I don't want you to go like that," I say.

"How do you want me to go?" she asks.

"Like this," I say, pushing myself into her. She arches again, moaning softly. I push into her over and over again and watch her face twist with pleasure. She digs her fingers into my back, and we are gone, both climbing, both focused on one thing.

"Oh my god," she says.

I feel her release and instantly react. I shudder and gasp and let myself go. I collapse into her. We wrap our arms around each other and I fall to the side, bringing her with me. Now we are lying side by side facing each other, a tangled mess.

"That was brilliant," she says. "Just brilliant."

"Agreed," I say, still catching my breath. We lie like this for a little while, my fingers stroking her neck and face. I don't know how much time goes by before she breaks the peaceful silence.

"Do you have to go?" she asks, careful not to point out why.

We both know. But I don't want to go. Not this time. I don't want to leave this place. "Actually, I can stay. If you want," I say.

She looks up at me and waits for more explanation.

I don't want to be too specific or too vague. "Her job has her away sometimes," I say, keeping it simple.

"Oh," she says, considering this information.

"I don't have to stay if you don't want," I say.

"No, it's not that. I want you to stay," she says. Her voice is unsteady.

"Are you sure? You seem hesitant."

"I just don't usually want people to stay," she admits.

Her words fill my chest up, as if in some way it had been hollow before. "Oh," I say, not sure what else to add. I pull her in closer to me and we fall back into silence for a little while longer.

"Can we get under the blanket?" she asks.

"Of course," I say, releasing my grip of her for the first time since we got into bed.

We shift around and wiggle our way under the blankets.

"I'm not going to make a big deal out of this, but I just want you to know you're on my side of the bed," she says, giving me a stern look.

"Well, I like it over here," I say, wiggling my body back and forth.

"Oh, I bet you do, it's obviously better," she says.

"Can I ask you a serious question?" I say.

"Sure," she says.

"Do you want to be the little spoon or the big spoon?" I say, staring into her eyes, pretending this is a very serious moment.

She pouts her lips, thinking about the question. "That's a very serious question indeed," she says. "I think tonight I'd like to be the little spoon if that's all right with you? I might want to be the big spoon another time."

"Deal," I say, positioning my body and wrapping my arm around her waist.

She wiggles her ass back into me and snuggles up. I can already feel myself getting distracted again. I shift.

"What's wrong?" she asks.

"You know on second thought, this may be a bad idea. I'm not sure I can sleep with your ass pushing back into my junk all night. It's very distracting. I'll end up being a very bad boy sometime in the middle of the night," I admit.

"Did you just call it your junk?" she asks, laughing.

"Well what do you want me to call it?" I ask.

"I don't know, I just never understood calling it junk. Isn't it more of a prized possession?"

"Oh, you bet it is," I say.

"As for the middle of the night bad behavior, I'm counting on it," she says and settles back down, giving her butt one last wiggle.

"Can I have a goodnight kiss?" I ask.

She turns toward me and plants her lips on mine squarely, deeply. It's not sexual, it's intimate. It's wonderful. She turns back and wiggles again. I inhale the scent lingering in her hair again and shut my eyes.

I lie there holding her and thinking. She seems to like me, and I wonder if I could tell her the truth. I wonder if a girl like her could find relief in my truth. I wonder if I've created a false sense of security with this lie. I wonder why I care so much. This is what I do right? Have some fun, call it quits later. The thought of doing that to Dani makes me feel sick. It makes me hurt. Why is this bothering me so much? What is so different about this time? *Her. It's her.* She's worth more than throwing away. Maybe this whole thing was a bad idea. In my head, it made perfect sense. She only dates married men. I am fake married. She's not stepping out of line, not wanting more. It's still early. Maybe she could want more. Maybe if I wait until then to tell her, she could be relieved. My thoughts begin to circle around, and I realize I'm getting nowhere. I know a few things to be true at this point.

Dani is different. I am afraid for the first time in a very long time. Afraid to hold on. Afraid to let go. Afraid of what the truth will do. Afraid of what my lie has already done.

17

MARK

Whoever she has over didn't leave this time. The lights went off in the living room and there's been no movement since. That fucker is sleeping there. That bitch said she never has dudes over and now one is spending the night? What the hell? Who the hell is this guy? I still haven't managed to get a good look at him. It's always dark out, and it's not like they linger.

I keep my eyes on her apartment for just a few minutes longer and realize nothing can be done tonight, yet again. Come hell or high water, she will pay. I take a swig from my flask and put it back into my pocket. I step out onto the sidewalk without fear of being seen. I turn to walk down the street toward my place and wipe the liquor from my lips on my sleeve. I walk just a few steps and see the bar where she works. I turn and stare at it while I smoke a cigarette. I can't believe this is where we met. So close to her place and yet I never knew. Sneaky bitch.

Maybe I can catch her at work. What did she used to say? She would go on break in the alley in the back? I remember her saying it was quiet back there, not many people back there. Maybe I could wait there. Yeah, I could snatch her up on a break. I could do that. It would be so easy. And I wouldn't have to worry about some dude showing up. It's not like he fucking follows her to work too.

That's what I'll do. I know when she usually works. It's probably dark back there too. I turn to keep walking and plot my plan. She'll never see it coming. I'll already have her by the time she realizes what is happening.

Perfect. Fucking perfect.

18

DANI

Lucas woke me up in the middle of the night with his lips. I didn't mind it. And while I could sit and pretend what happened before we fell back asleep was nothing more than drowsy sex, it was a bit more intimate than that, a bit more tender. My body reacted to his touch in a way I couldn't explain. Pleasure was one thing. Complete and utter openness and vulnerability was another.

The thought of letting myself go like that frightens me. But each time I think of Lucas, I smile, and it feels like it could be okay. I lie there beside him in bed in the early morning hours and watch him sleep. I push his hair back and don't remember a time I was this content with a man in bed. For me, it had always been about the sex. But this is more. I can feel it. I brush my hair back behind my ear and wonder if it feels like more to him too. Not that I had anything to compare this to. But it certainly feels different than say, Mark. That's something, right?

Of course, he doesn't feel something more. *He's fucking married, Dani. Why would you even think that? You know better.*

Married men never leave their wives. You're just here for fun. Nothing more. Although sometimes, I think I could be wrong.

Lucas shifts and stretches his arms out with his eyes still closed but I can tell he's awake.

"Good morning, you," I say.

"Good morning to you. How did you sleep?" he asks.

"Not too bad considering someone is on my side of the bed."

He laughs. "What time is it?"

"Just after seven," I reply.

He groans and throws his arm over his eyes. "I guess I have to go to work in a little while."

"You guess?"

"Yeah. Meaning I don't want to. Meaning I guess I will even though I'd much rather stay here and ravage you three more times before lunch," he says.

I gulp hard. "I mean I wouldn't complain."

"Don't tempt me. I will totally call in sick," he says.

I consider the notion for a moment and decide not to press it. "Can I ask you something?"

"Of course," he says.

"Well, I have a birthday coming up. It's in a few weeks. And maybe it's a little presumptuous, but would you want to come to my party? I have to have a party."

"You have to have a party? Like have to?" he asks.

I shift a little. "Yes. I have to."

"You're not going to tell me why?"

"Um, I'm not sure you'd want to know. It's heavy. You're here for fun, right?" I ask.

He shifts a bit and clears his throat. Something about his movement strikes me. He doesn't like my words.

"I mean, I guess you're right. But, like, you can talk to me, you know?" he says.

"I can? About the heavy stuff, you mean?"

"Yeah. Of course. You have to have somewhere to unload it. I can handle it, you know," he says.

I consider his words for several minutes. Is my past safe with him? "My mother is alive." I say, finally saying it out loud to someone.

His face jerks to look at mine. "Oh, I'm sorry, just the way you've spoken about her made me think otherwise."

"No, it's not your misunderstanding. I give that impression on purpose."

"Why?" he asks me.

"Because it's easier that way. Easier than this conversation."

"What's going on?"

"She's in prison. And she's never getting out," I say. Another thing I've never said out loud to someone else.

"Wow," he says. A look of shock rolls over him and I can tell he doesn't know what to say or what to ask.

"She saved my life, though, Lucas. I need you to know

that. She's there because of me. She's there because she protected me," I say.

"What happened, Dani? You can tell me," he urges, rubbing my shoulder.

"She was a prostitute, okay? She was a prostitute and a bad man came to our house when she wasn't home." I swallow hard. The next part hurts. "He touched me. He took my shirt off and he was touching me, and I was only eleven." I say. I feel Lucas's hand grip my shoulder harder. I can see his jaw clenching.

"I'm sorry, Dani," he says.

"My mother came home and saw what he was doing. She made me hide in my closet. She killed him. And she was just a prostitute and he was more important to this world. No one cared it was to protect me. No one cared she was just doing what any mother would. They sent her away," I say. I've never told anyone any of this. I swallow again, waiting for him to speak, expecting cruelty.

"That's awful, Dani. I'm so sorry you had to go through that. I'm so sorry she can't be here with you," he says softly.

He keeps rubbing my shoulder and I can feel tears well up in my eyes. I stand up from the bed and put my other robe around me. I can't do this here. I walk over to my closet and open the door. "Can you come here?" I ask him. I feel stupid but I can't stop myself.

He gets up from the bed and follows me to my closet. I sit down on the floor and gesture for him to sit beside me. He sits down and pushes himself back into the closet next to me. I don't say anything just yet. I let the tears fall.

"What are we doing in here, Dani?" he asks, stroking my hair.

And so, I explain it to him. I tell him about my castle as a kid. I tell him about how my mother put me in there, how it was to protect me. I tell him how despite being a hooker, she was the best mom. I tell him I haven't cried outside of a closet since I was a kid and that I still sit on the floor of one when I need to feel safe. He looks at me and presses his lips together. I don't feel judgment like I expect.

"That's okay, you know. I'm sure she was a really great mom. And it sounds like she'd do it all over again to protect you again. It's okay, Dani. Really. Thank you for telling me," he says.

I lay my head on his shoulder and sniffle a few more times. He sits there with me and lets me get it out. "I've never told anyone that before," I admit.

"None of it?" he asks.

I shake my head.

"Well, thank you for trusting me with it. I'll keep your secret safe," he says.

"That's why I have to have a party. She asked me to. She wants to see pictures. She's tired of me not celebrating it."

"You haven't celebrated your birthday? Ever?" he asks, shock in his voice.

"No," I say.

He shifts a little and leans up. "Okay, then you need an awesome party. Like a big one," he says, smiling at me.

Maybe it won't be so bad. Maybe with him there, I could enjoy it. "Okay," I say. "I'll have a party."

"Yes!" he shouts.

I laugh and wipe the tears from my eyes. "Do you need me to help you plan it?"

"That would be good, actually," he says.

I mentally settle into the fact that in a few short weeks I will be having a full-blown birthday bash with people and drinking and music and maybe even some gifts.

"Oh my god, wait," he says, the shock returning. "Does that mean you've never gotten a birthday present?"

"Not since I was eleven," I say. I didn't really think it was a big deal but the look on his face says otherwise.

"Okay, challenge accepted. I'm now in pursuit of the best, most perfect birthday gift," he says.

"You don't have to do that," I say.

"Oh yes, I do, Dani. I do," he says, pulling my chin up to look me in the eyes. He kisses me softly.

"I guess you should start thinking about going to work," I say, biting my bottom lip where the feel of his kiss is still lingering.

"Actually, I think I'd rather call in and take you on a day date. If you want?" he asks.

"Really?"

"Definitely," he says.

"Okay," I say, smiling.

"All right, I'm going to run home and change my clothes. You get ready, okay? I'll only be like half an hour," he says, getting up from the closet and getting dressed.

"Perfect," I say.

He kisses me at the door and walks out. I turn back to my bedroom to find something to wear. Without knowing where we are going, picking clothes might be a challenge but day dates are generally casual. I pull out some skinny jeans and a t-shirt. I'll wear my boots as always. I start getting ready and think about how kind Lucas had been to me this morning.

If I'm being honest, Lucas is starting to scare me. Not him, but his presence. The way he makes me feel. In our short time together so far, I always find myself looking forward to more. I think forward to my party. It will be nice to have him there. The friends I do have, they've never seen me with anyone. Quinn would be really surprised, considering I would never let her set me up.

After dressing and putting on some make-up, I turn my attention to cleaning the apartment. I need to distract myself from my distraction, if that makes sense. I need to think of anything other than Lucas. I need to think about something other than the fact that I wish he wasn't married. This isn't like me. The entire stream of thoughts I'm having are dangerous and strange. My mother's words echo in my head.

Be careful. You like him.

They're always going to hurt you.

They're never going to want you like you want them.

It's what they do. It's who they are. You can't change a cheater's nature.

Great. He'll be back any minute and my mind is heavy with wishing for the impossible.

I hear a knock at the door. Time for that day date.

"ARE YOU GOING TO TELL ME WHERE WE ARE GOING?" I ask.

"Nope," Lucas says.

I laugh. Of course, he wanted to surprise me. He likes his surprises. We are in his car heading east out of the city.

"Fine," I say. I cross my arms across my chest and pretend to pout.

He laughs at me. "Okay, okay, I'll give you a clue. There is water there."

"Well, we don't live near a beach, and you didn't tell me to pack a swimsuit, so that's limiting," I say, thinking hard about his clue.

"I think you'll like it," he says.

"I'm sure I will," I say. I plug my phone into his car and start scrolling through some songs until I find "Tiny Dancer" by Elton John and press play with possibly a little too much excitement. When the music starts, I begin to bounce in my seat a little and I notice Lucas eyeing me with a wide smile. "What?" I ask.

"Oh, nothing at all," he says.

"Are you laughing at me?" I ask, crossing my arms.

"Not even a little. You're adorable," he says.

"Well thank you," I say. I bop my head back and forth to the song and we go onward down the road.

We pull into the parking lot of the Newport Aquarium and my face lights up. "Oh my god, are we going to the aquarium?"

"Have you ever been?" he asks.

"Never!" I say.

"How is that possible?" he asks.

"I don't know, I've had a boring life I guess," I say.

"Well I'm fixing this one thing now at least," he says.

We get out of his car and start toward the entrance. We get in line at the ticket booth and I see couples and families all standing together in line. Sometimes when I see normal couples, I'm almost envious, but today I get to pretend I am in one.

Lucas puts his hand in mine and leads me through the line. He kisses the top of my head and whispers in my ear. I laugh and notice a few people looking at us. I can't help but wonder if they know, or if perhaps they saw us the way I look at other couples. Lucas pays for our tickets and we walk inside. I am so excited, I feel a bounce in my step, like a child half-skipping to her own party.

"What's your favorite sea creature?" he asks.

"Definitely the octopus," I say.

"How come?"

"When an octopus experiences turmoil, it will rip out all three of its hearts," I say.

"Wait, what?" he asks.

"It's a line I read once by a poet named Nikki Carroll. It sort of stuck with me. I can relate. It's sort of what I did with my life, you know? To protect myself," I say.

"Yeah, I get that," he says, and it sounds like he genuinely does.

"So, we definitely have to see them!" I say.

"Definitely," he says.

We wander through tube corridors and watch colorful fish swimming all around us until we get to the shark area and stop for a little while longer.

"This is by far one of the better tanks," I say, my eyes wide.

"I agree," he says.

I watch him as he watches a large shark swim over his head. The wonder of this place isn't just for children. We walk into the next area and it grows darker. Large tanks of bright jellyfish are all around. The lighting highlights all their tiny little features and for a second, I almost think about switching my earlier answer.

"Dani, this way," he says, holding his hand out to me.

We enter another dark room and there it is. A giant octopus is in a large tank in the center of the floor, stretching its tentacles outward toward the glass. I pause for a moment in shock before running up to the glass. I stand in awe, watching the majestic creature slink and glide through the water. I feel Lucas wrap his arm around my waist and pull me into him.

"Lucas, this is amazing," I say.

He kisses me on my temple, and I brush my hand across the hair on his jawline.

"I'm glad you like it," he says.

"I really do," I say.

We stand there watching the octopus for several more minutes before moving on to the next exhibits.

"Are you hungry?" Lucas asks, gesturing toward the café that's mid-way through the exhibits.

"Yeah, I could eat," I say.

We go through line and grab some turkey and swiss wraps, chips, and drinks. We find an unoccupied table near the corner and take a seat.

"So, I take it this will go down in your book as a good date?" Lucas asks.

"Well, I don't have a lot to compare it to, to be honest. I don't go on a lot of dates. But, of the few I've been on, this is by far the best one," I answer.

Lucas sits back, studying my face. "I just can't believe you haven't been on that many dates. Who wouldn't want to take you out?"

"Well, it's a combination of things really. One being that I don't accept many dates."

"Now I feel special," he says, putting his hand across his heart.

"You should," I say, laughing. I take another bite of my wrap and I hear him open his chips. The smile on his lips never leaves though.

We spend a few minutes eating in silence and clean up our trash.

"Ready to see the rest?" he asks.

"Definitely," I say.

We walk over to the section of the exhibits where you can stick your hand down into the water and pet different crustaceans.

"No way am I sticking my hand in there," Lucas says. He crosses his arms in front of him while I am elbow deep in the first tank.

"Oh, come on, they feel so cool!" I say, trying my best to convince him.

"Nope. No thank you," he says.

"Not even for a crisp hundred-dollar bill?" I push my bottom lip out and start pouting. "How about for a kiss?"

"Don't do that," he says.

"Do what?" I ask, pushing my lip out again.

"The puppy dog face thing," he says.

"But I'm not," I say. I push out my lip and make the biggest puppy dog eyes I can.

"Fine. You know what? Fine, I'll do it. But I want two kisses."

"Deal," I say, perking up. I love the smell of victory.

Lucas unfolds his arms slowly and approaches the tank I have my arm in. He peers down into the water and grimaces. He dips his fingers in and I see his shoulders tense up. "It's so cold," he says.

"Don't be such a wuss," I say.

He shoots a look in my direction and plunges his arm deeper into the water until his hand touches the same starfish mine is touching.

I smile the biggest smile I can manage.

"Don't do that," he says.

"What?" I ask.

"Grin at me, so pleased with yourself," he says.

"But I am."

"Oh, I know you are," he says.

We take turns touching more things in the tanks. I can't tell you what half of them are, but I am having a blast and Lucas is glad I'm having a blast. He isn't much for touching the things himself, though he is a good sport about it.

We reach the end of the aquarium and there is a gift shop. I shoot Lucas a "pretty please" look and he nods his head. I take him by the hand and drag him inside.

I'm looking at refrigerator magnets and keychains when Lucas walks up to me with a gift bag already in hand.

"I got you something," he says, looking pleased with himself.

"You did?" I ask, surprised and excited.

"Yep, but you'll have to wait until we get to the car," he says.

He holds his hand out to me and we walk out together, still on a happy high from the day. I check my phone for the first time and it's later than I thought.

"Wow, we were out all day," I say.

"I'm not complaining," he says.

"Oh, me neither. I'm just surprised."

We get to the car and he opens the door for me. I sit down inside, and he goes around to his side, sliding in next to me.

"You ready?" he asks.

"Ready!" I say.

He holds out the bag and I take it into my lap, opening the top. I remove the paper inside to find a large stuffed pink octopus. It's soft and adorable I want to laugh and cry at the same time.

"Do you like it?" he asks.

"Oh my god, I love it!" I say. "It's perfect and cute and ridiculous in the best way." I hug it to my chest and smile.

"Good, I'm glad," he says.

"This may be the best gift," I say.

"Well, that's because I haven't given you your birthday gift," he says, smirking.

"Stop it," I say.

Lucas pulls out of the parking lot and we head back. I put

on some soft music and we hold hands the entire way back, enjoying the music and a comfortable quiet between us.

Today Lucas had given me something so many had failed to do, something so many weren't even interested in doing actually. Today, we were just a normal couple. We went out on a regular date and did regular couple things. Now I had a pink octopus for my bed, a tangible memory to hold onto. Perhaps that wasn't the best idea, given this would all fall apart at some point. But I didn't care. I wanted to pretend, just for today.

Today, we were more. Today, we were something.

20

LUCAS

I've been seeing Dani for a few weeks now and her birthday is quickly approaching. I've been hunting for the perfect birthday gift, but I can't seem to find it. I have this feeling that when I see it, I will just know, but I haven't seen it yet. I'm determined to figure it out today. I've been walking from shop to shop, touching fabrics, looking at jewelry, smelling perfumes. Nothing's right.

Over the past few weeks, it became obvious to me I was falling for her. Hard. We spent a lot of time together, especially considering my brother had managed to cancel on me three more times and we still hadn't met up. Each time he canceled, I found myself at Dani's doorstep, wanting more of her, craving more of her. Sometimes I think I could make her happy. Like happy, happy. Sometimes I think I could tell her the truth and she wouldn't run, she wouldn't end it with me. Sometimes I think she could even be happy and excited. Sometimes I think she could love me. But then I remember who she is, I remember what she is made of, and I know in my heart she will run.

This is the entire fucking reason I have the life I do, the entire reason I wear this meaningless ring and go on like I do. To keep myself from this. I'm right back to where I never wanted to be. I'll probably get hurt soon. I shake the thoughts from my head. I go into the next shop and start the process over again when I get a text.

Dani: Hey you.

Me: Hello beautiful.

Dani: I have a question.

Me: Shoot.

Dani: I totally understand if this is too much, but would you want to come with me tomorrow to see my mother? She's the most important person to me. I just thought it would be nice. Maybe I'm crazy. Maybe it doesn't make any sense for you to come with me. I get it if it doesn't. She knows the situation. I tell her everything in my letters to her.

I'm taken aback for a moment, shocked at the question but not in a bad way. These are the kinds of moments that lead me to believe she could really want me beyond what she says.

Me: I would be honored to go with you.

Dani: Really? She says she wants to meet you. To talk about my birthday party. Haha.

Me: I'll be ready to talk about it then.

Dani: Coming over tonight?

Me: You bet. I can just stay and go with you tomorrow if that's okay?

Dani: You're the one with the schedule. If you're good, I'm always good.

Me: I'm good.

Pretending my wife is a nurse with a demanding schedule makes it easy enough to have as much free time as I want, really. But it doesn't stop Dani from reminding me of my other commitments occasionally. Perhaps she was reminding herself too. She was never mean about it. They were just gentle reminders of the rest of my life. The rest of my pathetic pretend life. My fake, fraudulent life. *God.*

Now I have two things to worry about. Dani's birthday present and meeting her mother tomorrow. I'm still pretty shaken she asked me. But if I'm being honest with myself, her mysterious mother is someone I'm very interested in meeting. It's just an intriguing story all the way around. At the very least, I could be a little less curious about her.

After another four stores I call it quits on the present search and head back to my apartment to collect my things for tonight's sleepover. I feel my phone go off again.

Elliott: Sorry I keep bailing. This side project is taking up all my time.

I roll my eyes. Of course. Maybe though…

Me: That's okay, man. This girl I'm seeing, her birthday is coming up next weekend. How about you make an appearance?

I'm surprised to see him apologizing for his lack of availability. That's real growth for him to be honest.

Elliott: Sounds good. Send me the info later.

Me: Will do.

I put my phone away and grab my stuff and throw it in a bag. I stop at the living room couch for a moment and see the vinyl in my living room. A light bulb goes off for me and I know what I have to do. I know the only thing I can do. I don't know why I didn't think of it before but it's perfect in a way nothing else could ever be. I grab my keys and make my way out the door.

Life has a funny way of showing you exactly what you need to see but not a moment before you need to see it. My theory was always that you saw it, but you didn't receive it as you needed to until you were meant to. This is how we learn lessons, or pass on lessons, or even accept something about ourselves we wouldn't before. I use this knowledge to try to be more receptive to my surroundings and events.

I pull up to Dani's apartment and step out onto the sidewalk, feeling a little uneasy. I don't know why exactly. Maybe I'm nervous. But I feel uncomfortable about something. I look around, up and down the streets and across the road but nothing feels out of place really. Not in an obvious way. I shake it off, certain it's just my mind playing tricks on me.

I get to Dani's door and knock but there's no answer. I knock again and wait. When she doesn't answer the second time, I call her phone and she picks up after a few rings.

Dani: Lucas?

Me: Dani? Where are you? I'm at your door.

Dani: Oh thank god, I'll be there in a second.

Her voice sounds shaky and I'm worried. She opens the door and we both put our phones away. She throws her arms around me and her entire body is shaking.

"What's wrong?" I ask, concerned something terrible has happened.

"Someone was trying to get into my apartment," she says.

"When?" I ask, panic in my voice.

"Just a few minutes ago."

"I didn't see anyone when I came up, they must've have gone quickly," I say.

"I don't know, I panicked and ran to my closet. They were saying my name through the door but they were disguising it on purpose. It really freaked me out," she says, clearly worried.

"Did you call the cops?" I ask.

"No," she says, putting her head down.

"Why not?" I ask, surprised.

"They took me away that night. All I remember are the blue lights. Cops frighten me and the blue lights trigger me. It's not their fault," she says.

I rub her back and pull her closer to me. I try to be understanding. "They're just doing their job. They're just here to help," I say, reassuring.

"I know."

"Promise me you will call them if something else happens," I say.

She hesitates and doesn't say anything.

"Promise me, Dani," I say to her.

"I promise," she finally says.

I hug her for a long time and try my best to calm her. "I'll run you a bath if you want," I say.

"No, I'm okay, really. Let's just go to bed," she says. She gets up from the couch and goes to the bedroom.

I pull my shoes off and strip down to my briefs. I watch her pull her shirt off and then her pants. Her hair falls just below her shoulders and brushes over her back. The tattoo on her thigh begs to be traced. I don't know why but, in this moment, I see her complete vulnerability, her delicate state of being. I watch her tuck her hair behind her ear. In this moment, I know I love her and I know we are destined to hurt each other. I regret everything, and nothing. I crawl into bed next to her and she looks up at me with a sweet smile. I kiss her lips and wrap my arms around her. I hold her tight, as tight as I can. One day I will have to let go, but today is not that day.

21
———

MARK

I've been watching her for weeks now. This guy in her life is always fucking around. I went into the alley at her work and hid behind some dumpsters but the few times I managed to see her back there, there was someone with her or someone too close to move in. This stalking thing takes a lot of fucking patience.

Tonight she was alone at her apartment so I tried to get to her. I tried knocking on the door and hiding out of sight of the peep hole. I disguised my voice but she didn't grow curious enough to open the door. I thought about trying to force the door open, but she has too many neighbors for that.

After a few minutes, I left. I figured if she wasn't answering she might have called the police or that guy she's seeing so it was best to get out of there fast.

No matter what, I will make sure it happens this week. I have to. I have to make sure of it. I can't keep doing this shit. I need to put her behind me and I can't do that until I get what I need, until I get her back for what she did to me.

No one says no to Marcus Elliott Stone and she needs to know that. I have to make her see. She has to pay.

22

DANI

I WAKE UP THE NEXT MORNING STILL WRAPPED UP IN Lucas's arms, so comfortable I would probably fall back asleep if I lie here too long.

"Good morning you," he whispers into my ear.

I feel his hands start to move over my body. We like taking each other in the morning. It's the best way to start the day. "Good morning to you, lover," I reply. I pull him on top of me and feel him begin to move against me. He kisses my neck because we both understand there's nothing sexy about morning breath. My hands rub his back. I've come to enjoy this morning ritual. We've carved out these few moments of lazy, slow morning sex each time he's spent the night and each time my day has always been better.

I can feel him inside me now and I begin to moan against his collarbone. I kiss and bite him. The pace quickens and I spiral out of control. After he finishes, he gets up to shower and leaves me on the bed.

"Are you coming to shower?" he asks.

"I'll be there in just a second. Still basking," I say.

He leaves the room and I hear him start the water. I close my eyes and steady my breath for a few minutes, relaxing in the aftermath of my orgasm. A smile spreads across my lips and against my better judgment, I know these days we make love more than we fuck. We both know it and we've both ignored saying anything about it. But I don't feel like this after meaningless sex. I've never felt like this with a guy. A married man. I can't pretend anymore. Not that I could do anything about it. I knew the deal. Married men never leave their wives, I remind myself. I knew that. I could pretend though, couldn't I? I could imagine the possibilities. I could close my eyes every once in a while, and dream of a different life.

Is this what love is? It's not like I had ever let myself feel it for a man. Is this aching for another what people call love? Perhaps going to meet my mother is a bad idea. Perhaps this whole thing is a bad idea. I have to start thinking about ending it soon. For my sake. I brush the thoughts away and head for the bathroom.

"There you are," he says.

"Here I am," I say, smiling. I climb into the hot shower and my shoulders slump.

"Want me to help wash you?" he asks, grinning.

"I wouldn't have it any other way," I say.

He takes the loofa and lathers it in his hands. He starts rubbing it over my back and neck first, taking his time. "Turn please," he says.

I oblige. "Can I ask you something?"

"Of course," he says.

"What happened between you and your brother? I know you said you had a falling out but you never said what it was about. You did say it was a later date thing, and I think it's safe to say we are past that."

Lucas falls silent for several minutes.

"Sorry, you don't have to answer," I say. "I didn't mean to drudge up something you didn't want to talk about."

"No, no, it's okay. Look, I don't want to go into the details right now, but I'll say this. He betrayed me. In a really big way. A way I never would have thought a brother would. I haven't spoken to him since then until recently, while trying to mend things. After my mom died, I realized he's the only family I have," he says.

I brush his wet hair clinging to his face away. "I'm sorry you had to deal with that."

"It's okay," he says.

"Can I ask you something else?" I ask.

"Sure."

"What does it feel like to fall in love?" I ask.

His eyes shoot up to meet mine. He keeps washing my breasts and shoulders, but there's surprise in his face. "You've never been in love?"

"Well, no not really. I designed my life so that I wouldn't." I say.

He lets my words sink in for a moment. "Well, um, it's difficult to explain. When it happens the first time, it's like everything else sort of falls away, seems less important, and you want to spend all your time with them and it doesn't feel like too much. It always feels like not enough. And you put them before yourself. Their happiness, everything. And nothing really makes sense, there's no why. Why doesn't exist. You just do. You'd do anything for them. You'd die for them. There's a warmth that radiates throughout your body even when you're just thinking about them and you know they're responsible for it. And you want to be a better person for them. You want to do better for them." His words trail off. "I'm not explaining it right."

"What do you mean?" I ask.

"Falling in love feels like exactly that. You're falling. And it's out of your control and there's nothing you can do to stop it and you're scared and you're at peace and you want to laugh and cry and you want to reach for a lifeline but you're pretty sure falling is the lifeline. You know nothing will ever be the same. And you're just praying the other person feels the same way. You're praying they're going to take your heart and tuck it safely into their chest. Because that's where it belongs now." He rinses the soap from me and lets me rinse my hair.

I think about his words for a little while. "How many times have you been in love?" I ask him.

He presses his lips together. "Just twice," he says.

"So you're pretty protective of yourself then," I say.

"Pretty much," he says.

Just twice. His wife and I wonder who else? I wonder who else captured his heart. I imagine for a moment it could be me even though I know better. Life is not that kind to me.

We towel off in silence and get dressed. We grab some

breakfast before we head out. He insists we take his car instead of the bus since he has one and so we get in and prepare ourselves for the ride.

"So how come you don't have a car for things like this at least?" he asks.

"I just don't see a point in it. Everything I need is so close, aside from my mother. I can just take the bus to her. No real reason to have one," I say.

"Fair enough," he says.

I'm surprised by his willingness to accept my answer rather than hound me with a ton of follow-up questions like most people. This is one of the things I like about Lucas. He doesn't push. He just accepts information for what it is. "I like that you're driving and I can just stare at you as much as I want," I say playfully.

He laughs at me. "Well, I am pretty good looking," he boasts.

"You're okay. Almost as good looking as I am."

This is us in a nutshell. We like to play and tease. It's easy. It's fun. I've never experienced this before. As much as I've sought it out, this is the first time I've actually found it. Lucas makes it easy. He doesn't know it but he makes it too easy. Because I think I'm falling and I don't think there's anything I can do about it now.

23

LUCAS

We head out of the city, northbound toward her mother, and I'm nervous. The last time I met a mother, it was when I got engaged. Not that I could tell her any of that. For all she knew, I'd met plenty of mothers, including my wife's. Today probably isn't the day to tell her the truth either. I didn't know exactly why her mother wanted to talk to me anyway. Wanting to talk to me about Dani's birthday seemed strange. I guess I'd find out.

"So, is she going to threaten to kill me if I hurt you or something?" I ask.

She laughs. "I doubt it. I mean she knows you're married so I don't know why she would approach you like that. She's never met anyone I've ever dated or seen. Maybe she's just having a moment of wanting to be really motherly. I'm not sure."

"Well, I'll try my best to impress," I say.

"Just be yourself," she says, smiling at me.

She weaves her fingers into mine and settles back into her seat as we settle into the drive. We fill the time with bits of conversation, spans of comfortable silence, and of course only the best curated music until we arrive at the gates of the prison. We park and get out.

"Leave your stuff here. Just take your license. It's easier," she says.

I take my ID out and leave my wallet in the car with my keys and phone. She takes hers out and leaves her purse and phone behind. I walk around the car to her and she takes my hand.

"You ready?" I ask her.

She nods her head. "Are you?"

"I wouldn't want to be anywhere else," I say, smiling at her.

We walk to the gate and make our way through checking in and presenting our licenses. Dani shows me the way and goes first through the whole process. We get to the end leading into the courtyard and she stops for a moment. She takes me by the hand again and squeezes it. She lets go just as quickly and walks to a woman in the back-right corner. For whatever reason, her mother isn't at all what I expected.

Her mother, Charlotte, is a small woman. Her slender shoulders and narrow hips do not paint her as a murderer, or a prostitute for that matter. In my mind, she was shapelier, more voluptuous. Her long graying hair is neatly braided and pulled to the side. Her eyes are as striking as her daughter's. Even with just this first meeting, she carries herself with an air of sophistication. I wonder to myself how a woman like her became a prostitute to begin with. Survival, I suppose.

"Mom, this is Lucas. Lucas, this is my mom, Charlotte," Dani says, smiling and glancing first to her mother and then to me.

"Ma'am, it's so nice to meet you," I say. "Dani has told me some lovely things about you."

Charlotte looks at me and squints a little, taking my hand in hers to shake. "Hello, Lucas. Dani has told me many things about you as well," she says.

Her reply isn't quite as warm as I expect, her tone flat and level. I'm caught off guard. Dani shifts. Perhaps she is too. We all sit; Dani and I on one side, Charlotte on the other.

"How has your week been, Mom?" Dani asks, shifting the conversation.

"Same as always. I can't complain," Charlotte says. Her eyes keep shifting to me as if she's searching me for something I don't think I have. Then she looks back at Dani. "How about you, princess?" she asks her.

"It's been okay, except someone tried to break into my apartment, I think," Dani says.

Her mother shoots a look in her direction, taking her eyes from me completely. "What happened?" she asks Dani, alarmed.

"I'm okay," Dani says. "Lucas showed up right after and I haven't really noticed anything else."

Charlotte looks at me again then back at her daughter. "Well, just be careful," she says to Dani.

"You know I am," Dani says.

Up to this point, I've just been quiet, not wanting to interrupt their moment, but Charlotte shifts her entire body in my direction and I know it's coming.

"So, Lucas. Dani tells me you're married. Don't worry, I'm not going to drill you about it. I understand the dynamic. But I have just one question," she says to me.

"Okay," I say, hesitantly.

"How many Danis have there been?" Charlotte asks me.

"Mom!" Dani says. "Lucas, you don't have to answer that."

"No, it's okay, I can appreciate the question." I pause for a moment, collecting my thoughts. "The truth is a bit more complicated. But the honest answer is a few and none. And I know what you're thinking. But what I mean is, yes, I've seen other women, but none like Dani," I say.

Charlotte squints at me again and her expression is stone cold. She turns to Dani. "Dani, my love, can you give us just a moment? I need to speak with him alone. About your birthday too," Charlotte says.

Dani hesitates for a few moments. I grab her hand beneath the table and squeeze it. I smile at her. She gets up and walks to the entrance of the courtyard.

"Listen, Lucas. You seem like a very nice man but I'm just a little confused. You and I both know a married man would never be meeting the mother of a woman he's seeing on the side. Let alone making a forty-five-minute drive north to meet one in prison. Come on, what gives?" she asks. She pulls no punches. Just like her daughter.

"I mean, I don't really know what to say, I just like her." I offer. I think I'm starting to sweat. My tongue feels thick and everything is sticky. She's staring at me and she's calling me out and I feel like the collar of my shirt is rapidly tightening.

"Married men don't leave their wives, Lucas. So you're either stringing Dani along or you're entertaining an idea you're never going to have the guts to go through with, but either way my Dani gets hurt and I can't allow that." She crosses her arms on the table in front of her and shifts her weight forward. Somehow it feels like she's towering over me despite being smaller than me in every way.

"Well, it's a little more complicated than that, ma'am, I um…"

She cuts me off. "Don't call me ma'am. I'm Charlotte. And you're not good for my daughter. Now I don't know what's happened but for whatever reason she seems to have fallen for you. She doesn't do that, which makes it even worse. Because you're going to leave."

"Look, I mean no disrespect, but you don't know my intentions," I say.

"Oh yeah? Look, I know this game. Let me tell you a little story, Lucas. My first John was a married man. I fell in love with him despite the warnings I received. I fell hard. He said he loved me too. He said he was going to leave his wife for me. And you know what happened? I got pregnant with Dani. And guess what? I never heard from him again. So don't tell me about intentions. Don't tell me about what men plan to do and what married men want. Because you all want the same thing. You want to have your cake and eat it too," she says. She sits back and smiles, I assume for Dani's sake.

"I don't know what to say," I say.

"You don't have to say anything. Here's what's going to happen. You're going to give my baby girl a birthday to remember because she's never had one. You're going to make it the very best you can because I can't. And she deserves it. And you'll go on for a time and then you'll end it because it's what you planned on doing anyway. But do it sooner rather than later, Lucas. For her sake. Don't let her fall too much further. Don't make healing be any harder than it already will be," she says.

I nod my head because I don't know what else to do. Charlotte straightens up and I feel Dani's hand on my shoulder. I put a smile on quickly and shift my body language to try to feel more positive.

We finish our visit and Dani hugs her mother. I shake Charlotte's hand again and she squeezes it—a reminder of the private conversation we'd just had. Dani and I walk back to the car in silence, holding hands. She has her head on my shoulder and I can tell she's a little bit sad to be leaving her mother. We reach the car and get in.

"Well?" she asks.

"Well what?" I ask.

"What did she want to talk to you about?"

"Oh she was just being motherly. Just intentions and your birthday. You know," I lie.

Dani looks and me and tilts her head. I try smiling to ease her worry, but she looks like she can see through me.

"I don't believe you," she says.

"Really, it was nothing, I promise," I say. I reach over and kiss her lips then turn and start the car. I back out and we start our drive back to the city.

There are more patches of silence on the ride back. Both of us are in our separate clouds of thoughts for most of the drive. I steal glances of Dani staring out the window and I leave her alone to think about her mother. I know what it must be like to miss her the way she does.

And I'm left alone to think about Charlotte's words.

In so many ways, she's right. I'm not good for Dani. Or good enough for that matter. I hate myself for that. I hate myself for lying to her. I hate myself for this lie. *What have I done?*

I look over at Dani again and realize all I had ever wanted to do was make her happy, see her laugh. I think of the first time I heard her laugh. I think about how I told myself I'd do anything to hear it again. How I wanted to be the source of it. Now, I have to come to terms with the fact that I would be the source of her pain. I was going to make her hurt. How would I live with myself after such a thing?

Maybe her mother is right. Maybe sooner would be better. Maybe it would be easier in some ways. Maybe it would hurt a little less.

We pull up in front of Dani's apartment and I put the car in park.

She turns to look at me. "I'm sorry," she says.

I shake my head. "What for?"

"For my mother. For what she said, how she acted," she says.

"Don't worry about it. She's just being a mom," I offer.

She nods and opens the car door.

I get out and come around to the sidewalk. I put my arms around her and she leans into my chest, wrapping her arms around me.

"Are you staying tonight?" she asks.

Her question sounds like a plea. I can feel how badly she wants me to. I hesitate for a moment, not sure if I should anymore. Or ever again. But the rest of my week leading up to her birthday was going to be pretty busy so maybe I should tonight. It might be the only chance I get to this week.

"I can tonight. The rest of the week I may not be able to," I warn.

She nods, understanding.

I take her hand and we walk to her door together. We get into her apartment and I am filled with the urge to have her again one last time in case it is the last time. In case I never get to touch her like this again.

I make love to her. I could call it something else but it would be a lie. I take my time with her. I kiss every inch of her skin. I savor every noise from her mouth. I want her to remember this. I want her to remember me. I will miss her.

24

DANI

After Lucas leaves, I clean my apartment and get ready for work. I'm working a double shift today to cover for someone and have to go in extra early. I lock my apartment and head downstairs. I walk in and wave to Quinn.

"Are you okay?" she asks.

I look around. "Yeah, why?" I ask.

"Well, you're not late, for one," she says.

I laugh and shake my head. "Yeah, I'm fine. Just Lucas on the brain," I admit.

I'd filled Quinn in every chance I got and she could tell I was smitten. That's what she called it. She enjoyed teasing me. Since I was early I stepped to the back and texted Lucas.

Me: Just got to work and already dreading the day. I'll be thinking of you.

I wait a few minutes but don't get a text back before I have to put my phone away and start my shift. It wasn't like him. He's usually pretty quick to respond. He's probably just busy, I tell myself. I tie my apron around my waist and get busy behind the bar with the lunch rush. I'm always surprised at how many people actually indulge in alcohol with their lunch. But I'm not complaining. They keep me busy.

"So, what's the plan for your birthday?" Quinn asks.

"Well, I think it's going to be at this place a few blocks over that Lucas picked. He says it's really fun," I reply.

"Can I bring the guy I'm seeing?" Quinn asks.

"Of course!" I say.

Quinn's been seeing the same guy for a while now, which is a relief. After a string of duds, this one finally seems to be worth keeping around. I'm happy for her.

The shift begins to slow down after lunch and before dinner so we take turns taking our breaks. Quinn comes back and I step outside to check my phone. Still no response from Lucas.

Me: Everything okay?

Lucas: Yeah, just really busy. Hope your night is going okay.

Me: It could be better.

I wait for more but get nothing. He's unusually quiet today and it worries me. Maybe whatever my mother had said to him is bothering him. I couldn't be sure. Maybe he really is busy with work. Just then, a rustling interrupts my thoughts and my eyes dart across the alleyway to the dumpsters. The lights above them went out months ago and have yet to be replaced so they're hard to see. I wait for more movement but hear nothing else. I squint to try to see more but I can barely make out the edges of the dumpsters themselves.

Me: Well, my break is over. Gotta get back in there.

Lucas: All right. Don't work too hard.

His words are short and nothing like the warm and flirty Lucas I'm used to. I try to brush it off, to not let it bother me too much but I can't help it. I come back in to the very beginning of the dinner hour starting and see a few familiar faces. Part of me can't help but hope that maybe Lucas will show up and surprise me. Maybe he'll apologize for his shortness or offer some sort of explanation later. He did mention he wouldn't be able to stay the night this week though so I doubt he'll be showing up. My mind begins running wild with thoughts. Thoughts I don't particularly care for. It wasn't enough that I had actually fallen for a married man, something I thought I would never do. But now, he might actually be starting to push me away and while I should have expected that, I just didn't see it coming. And with my birthday coming up? I just didn't see that from Lucas. He wouldn't do that. There's definitely an explanation for this. I'm sure of it.

I finish up the dinner rush and take another break out back. This time one of the dishwashers is out there too.

Me: This day is almost over! How about yours?

Lucas: Finishing up too.

I hesitate and then take a chance on calling him. It rings twice and then he picks up.

"Hey you," he says. He sounds a bit more like himself.

And I exhale, realizing I had been holding my breath. "Hey, how are you?" I ask.

"So tired, honestly. I had a long day at work. Plus, finalizing some birthday things, of course. I'm going to send you the name of the place and time of the party for you to pass on to the people you want to invite. Sound good?"

"Yeah, that's fine." I say.

"Oh and I invited my brother," he says. "He will probably bring his wife. I hope that's okay?"

"Yeah, totally," I reply. The line is silent for a moment.

"Okay, well I better go. I'm almost home," he says.

"Right, okay. Talk to you later," I say.

"Bye you," he says.

"Bye," I say. I hang up the phone and for the first time since we've been seeing each other, I feel like the other woman. For the first time, possibly ever, I feel ashamed about what I'm doing, about who I am. In his tone, in his words, he's somehow managed to make me feel bad. I don't have another word for it. I feel bad. I feel small.

I put my phone away and go back in to clean up. I make the short walk home and upstairs and given what's happened, I don't take my time. I get into my apartment and lock the door behind me quickly. I'm not sure what I would do if something like what happened before happened again. I don't think I could count on Lucas. I don't think I could manage to call the police. Maybe I could call Robert downstairs. He's so old though, what would he do?

I shake the thoughts from my head and walk to my closet

to change my clothes. I kick off my boots and peel out of my work clothes. I throw on an oversized t-shirt and stand in front of my closet for a moment, holding the door open. I stare into the back of it and let my mind wander the way it does to moments when that was the safest place I could recall. I take a step forward. I see flashes in my mind. Me as a little girl. My mother's nightgown. I take another step into my closet. I pull a blanket from the top shelf. I see a small pink flashlight in my mind. I hear men's voices. I can smell my mother's perfume. Her cigarettes. I see blue lights. I sit and close the door. I wrap myself in the blanket and I can feel the rush of tears coming. I try with all I have to hold them back but there's no escaping them. I am crying without understanding what brought it on.

I think of Lucas but that doesn't halt the tears. I let myself feel everything I have been avoiding. I let myself drown in my emotions. Up to this point, I had only scratched the surface. I had merely entertained a fraction of what he made me feel. He opened me up. I was exposed now. And because of that, I knew he had the power to wound me. I knew I had given him the weapons to destroy me. And what's worse, I knew he would. It was only a matter of when, not if. This was the way it was meant to be after all. This was the only outcome there could be. It's been written since the beginning.

I fall asleep on the floor of my closet. I wish I could say it was the first time. Tears dry down my cheeks. In so many ways, this is more comfortable and feels safer than my own bed. My own brokenness is not lost on me. What sort of person feels safest hulled up on the floor of her closet? What sort of woman only fucking dates married men? The broken kind. The kind with no past to speak of. The kind with no future to want.

25

LUCAS

I feel like a complete ass for lying to Dani. I mean the big lie was one thing but now the smaller lie of avoiding seeing her because I think I'm having an existential crisis. Her mother's words to me are all I can think about. Make no mistake about it, Dani is smart and she came from smart stock. Maybe she's right. What is the end of this? Come clean with Dani and expose myself as possibly the biggest fraud she's ever known or leave her? Either way I lose her. The question is, which does less damage in the long run? What makes it easier for Dani to move on?

I can only avoid her for so long. Her birthday is soon and preparations for it are well underway. Things are in motion. I have to make it good, really good. Charlotte was definitely right about one thing. Dani does deserve a great birthday for once in her life. I can give her that. If for no other reason than I have to bail anyway, I will do that for her. Hopefully, in some small way, she can remember that instead of what will follow.

I lied to Dani about working today in order to stay at home and plan. Plus, I'm not quite sure I can face her just yet. I'm still on the fence about seeing her later. I worry how my being suddenly less available is looking to her and making her feel but I can't help it. I don't exactly want the next time I saw her to be her birthday party either so I know I have to see her soon.

I make a series of calls to the venue about food and drinks and reserving their entire back room for plenty of space and more privacy than just being in the general population. For an additional fee, they also take care of some light decorating. What is a birthday party without balloons and confetti after all? Given the importance of the event, I chose rose gold. I figured I couldn't go wrong with such a fancy color. I know if Dani had it her way, everything would be black, but I just couldn't let that happen this time.

She gave me a small list of people she invited including some present and former coworkers and a neighbor named Robert. When I called him to confirm, he sounded old which threw me off guard but it's her party and her list so he's going to be there. She asked me to ask everyone not to bring her birthday presents but I completely ignored that request and everyone I spoke to agreed as well. I'm not sure how I'd feel about a birthday party with no gifts. I don't think I would be doing her justice. Amidst my planning, my phone buzzes.

Dani: How's work?

Me: Not bad, just trucking along.

Dani: Is it going to be a long day?

Me: Probably not too bad actually.

I knew she was poking to see if I would be coming over later. I'm just not sure what to say yet.

Dani: Well that's good. Any plans later?

There it is. I stare at my phone for a few seconds and think about it.

Me: No, I can come over later if you want.

Dani: That sounds good.

Me: Okay. I'll let you know when I'm on my way.

Dani: Great.

I turn my thoughts back to planning and check my list. I'm fairly certain I'm not forgetting anything. I ordered a cake from the bakery just two shops down from the venue so I'd just have to pick it up and deliver it beforehand. There's really nothing else left to do.

I have a few hours to kill before I go over to Dani's and I have no idea what to do with them. Other than to agonize over what my gift to her would be. I haven't figured it out yet and it's been driving me crazy. I thought for sure I would be able to come up with an idea pretty easily but everything that has popped into my mind didn't feel good enough. Given her interest in music, I considered concert tickets but backed out of the idea after speaking to her mom. I couldn't exactly only get her one ticket and if I got tickets for both of us, I would have to go with her and who knows when that would be? Maybe it would be too much at that point. Too much time, too much invested. I have to keep thinking but I'm running out of time.

I shift my focus again on going to see Dani. I check the time and decide to mix it up tonight. Instead of driving over there, it might be nice to clear my head on a walk. After all, she isn't even really that far if I cut through the park like before. I pack a backpack with what I need and put on more suitable walking attire. Maybe a brisk walk in the evening air would help me. I text her to let her know I'm on my way and she tells me she's ordering in food which is perfect because I'm getting hungry.

I lock my door and head out, making the familiar turns. I see the park ahead and have a strange thought. I have to get there before I can do anything about it. I walk into the park and find a bench toward the center. The park is long and trails go all over it. I hope this will work or it won't be nearly as romantic. I take out my phone and send Dani my location.

Me: Put on your walking shoes and come find me.

Dani: Really? Haha, okay see you soon.

I sit on the bench scrolling through Dani's playlist she'd given me weeks ago and listen to my favorite picks over again. Maybe I can sit here with her for a while and listen to this song we kissed to. Maybe I can look her in the eyes and tell her what I've done, the lie I've told. Maybe. I've never managed to do it before but Dani's different and she'll surely walk away from me once she hears it but for some reason the truth is the only thing I've wanted to tell her since I met her.

I look around the park. The crowds have thinned and only a few remain. A couple is sitting a way's down the path to the left of me on another bench. If I had to guess, I'd bet it was early. Only a few dates in. They are flirtatious but still nervous. The way so many of us are when we're wondering what this is and if it will stick and where it's going. We don't want to say the wrong thing and we don't want to misstep. We're full of hope or fear all at once. Especially when we really like the other person. New feelings can be paralyzing and freeing all at once.

"Hey you."

Dani's voice interrupts my thoughts and I shake them from my mind, turning my attention to her. I look up and smile. She approaches me and leans over to kiss me. I pull her in for a split second and have her sit next to me.

"I'm just doing some people watching. What do you think of them?" I ask her, pointing to the couple I had been examining. I watch her bite her bottom lip a little and tilt her head to the right. Her deep thought face is adorable. Everything about her is adorable.

"Well, I'd say it's early but not too early. Not first date but not twentieth either," she says, sitting back against my arm. She looks up at my face, waiting for my opinion.

"That was my assessment as well," I say, smiling.

"Okay, let me pick one now," she says, rubbing her hands together. She scans the few other people in the park, looking for the perfect subjects for such an experiment. "Her. What about her?"

My eyes meet the woman hers are fixed on. She's sitting alone with a book in her hand. I can't tell what book it is from here and I don't see a ring on her hand or a sign of a spouse. "Definitely single. She's lonely. She reads to get away. In the park so she can watch other people. Maybe on some days so she doesn't feel so alone. Maybe on others so she can watch them and envy what they have," I say.

"Well that's depressing," she says, laughing. "But I don't think you're right."

"Well, then you tell me," I say, challenging her to perk up the situation.

She turns her eyes back to the woman reading on the patch of grass a little way's away. She studies her for a few silent moments. "I think you're right about her being single but I think you're wrong about how she feels about it. I think she wants it that way. At least for now."

"Why do you say that?"

"Because I know what that's like. Because I just get it," she says.

I'm not sure how to respond now. I wonder if this is her way of telling her me she likes her life the way it is, that she doesn't want me to mess it up. I wonder if this is her way of holding up a caution sign without actually having to say anything about us at all. Perhaps the truth isn't what she wants after all.

"You feel like taking a little walk before we go back to your place?" I ask.

"Sure," she says, smiling.

"Good." I smile back. I take her by the hand and lead her down the path away from her place.

"I have a song for you," she says.

"Oh yeah?"

"Yeah. Here, put this in your ear." She hands me one of her ear buds and slips the other one into her ear so we can share the song.

I watch her scroll through her songs and stop on "Looking for Knives" by DYAN. She pushes play and looks up at me. It's soft, mellow. The lyrics though. The lyrics are undeniably amazing. This may be the best song she's had me listen to. The more I listen, the more I realize this song could have been written for us. What I went looking for versus what I was given. I look down at her and smile. *Wait. Is she trying to tell me something with this? Is this how she feels? Shit.*

Perhaps I would do this with everything now. Read too much into everything that happens between us and never know what she's thinking. Great. That's exactly what I need right now.

I take the turn out of the park toward my apartment and watch her look around, curiosity in her wondering eyes. I stop a little short of my place but make sure it is clearly visible. I pull the ear buds out and point at my building.

"Dani, do you see that place right there? White building, blue door?" I ask.

"Yes."

"That's where I live," I say.

Her face looks up at mine.

"I just…I just want you to know. In case you ever need to find me," I say.

"Why would I need to find you there?" she asks.

"You never know," I say. I'm not sure what I'm trying to accomplish. I'm not sure what she would even do with this information.

"Okay, Lucas. I'll know where to find you," she says, squeezing my hand in hers and smiling.

We turn back toward the park and put the ear buds back in. She scrolls through to find us another song. She picks "Broken" by lovelytheband and we both laugh. We take the winding paths through the park and walk down the street to her door where a delivery guy is standing. We may have forgotten about the food but it seems we aren't all too late to receive it. We bring it upstairs with us and sit it on the counter. I take my bag into her bedroom and come back out to eat.

"Lucas?" she says.

"Yeah?"

"Do you think if we were normal, we would have dated?"

"If we were normal?" I twist my face.

"You know what I mean," she says.

I consider it for a moment. I know what she means. She means normal circumstances. She means if she was just a girl and I was just a boy and we had maybe just seen each other across a coffee shop. She means if we weren't such fucked up people with skewed views of love and commitment and marriage.

"Honestly?" I say.

"Of course," she says.

I hold my breath for a moment. "I think we could have been great," I say.

She presses her lips together, tilts her head a bit, and nods. In agreement or acknowledgment, I don't know. We are both quiet after that. We settle into eating the way we have so many times before and for a little while I let myself pretend we are normal. I let myself pretend there is no lie and no truth to keep or tell. I sit and eat and for these minutes, we are a real couple. I smile at her and she smiles back.

That's what I'll do tonight. Pretend we are something we're not. Pretend we are everything I've been running from.

26

DANI

I SIT ACROSS FROM HIM TAKING BITES OF TAKEOUT I BARELY want now. My body is hungry but my mind is distracted. Tonight has been strange. Not in a bad way. Not in a good way. Maybe bittersweet is the right word. I still don't understand why he showed me where he lives but it seemed special. Like maybe he didn't let everyone in my position see it. That's what I want to believe anyway.

"Do you want to take a shower after this?" I ask, breaking the silence.

"That sounds really good actually. A long one, if that's all right," he says.

He takes another bite and he seems distracted too but I don't ask. I'm afraid of what the answer would be. I can't help but wonder if the guilt of our situation is getting to him. Wouldn't it for some? I wouldn't know. Though sometimes I do have a little guilt on my end. Perhaps some men are capable of it too then. Not all, but some. Not even most, but maybe a few. I think Lucas could be one of them. It's only a matter of time really. Until he leaves. I know this.

I watch him push his plate away after a few more bites and rest his chin on his palm while he stares in my direction. This is his not-so-subtle way of telling me to hurry up. I giggle at his expressions and take one last bite before pushing my plate away. I stand slowly and he does the same. I walk the few paces between us and his arms find my waist. I reach up around his neck and run my fingers through the short hair on the back of his neck. He leans down and kisses me gently on my lips. We walk to the bathroom together and I pull his shirt over his head. He returns the favor and then I remove his pants. And we go on like this, back and forth, until we are both completely naked. We stand there looking at each other, soaking it in the way we usually do. Bath time has become somewhat of a ritual between us. I lean over to start the water.

"I know we said a shower but can we start with a bath? Bubbles too?" Lucas asks.

I nod and plug the drain. I add bath salts, bubble bath, and a bomb. My mother called this "the bath time trifecta".

"I see you've come around to liking baths," I say.

"I mean they're pretty good. The wet naked lady helps too," he says.

When the water is halfway up the side we step in, facing each other, and we sit down. He puts his legs on either side of me and I put my legs over his thighs. This is how we fit, perfectly snug. We lean back and relax our bodies into the water filling around us. Lucas takes my foot in his hands and begins rubbing the sole.

I let out an audible moan. "That feels amazing," I say. I shut my eyes and even with them closed, I know he's watching my face rather than what his hands are doing. I don't know why he does this. Perhaps he's watching to see if I have any physical responses or a change in expression. Perhaps he likes the way my face looks in that moment, totally relaxed. Knowing him, it's a bit of both.

"I know you said you didn't want a birthday present but you know I'm getting you something right?" Lucas says.

My eyes shoot open. "No," I say.

"Yes."

"But, no," I respond.

"But, yes," he says back.

"I'm not going to win, am I?" I ask.

"What kind of person would I be if I was trying to throw you the best birthday and there was no gift?" he asks.

He has a point. I'm not sure my mother would side with me on this either. "Fine, okay. Just please don't spend a lot," I plead.

"I will spend what I need to," he says.

"That sounds unusually cryptic," I say, grimacing.

"It was meant to."

I roll my eyes. I can't win this. I know I can't and so I shrug my shoulders and lean back into the tub again. "Fine. Just keep rubbing."

"Rude," he says.

"I respectfully disagree," I say, teasing.

He grabs the other foot and starts rubbing deep into the center. I arch my foot in response and think I could die happy right here in this moment.

"You're lucky you're cute," he says.

"You're lucky I'm cute too," I say with a laugh.

"Someone is in a mood," he says.

"I can't help myself sometimes. I'm just so good." I lean up and pull my foot from his hands. I shift my body weight and straddle him. I put my arms around his neck and smile down at him.

"That you are," he says.

He pulls me down closer and pushes the hair from my face. He tucks strands behind my ears and stops. He pauses for a long moment, just staring into my eyes and I don't realize I'm holding my breath until he kisses my mouth and I begin to breathe again. He puts his arms around me and kisses me deeper. I'm almost certain I could never tire of kissing him.

I pull back from his lips and our breathing is heavy, our eyelids the same. I can never tell what he's thinking in these moments but I want to know.

"What are you thinking right now?" I ask.

He rubs his bottom lip with his thumb.

I sit up a little, putting more space between us.

"I'm thinking sad things. I'm thinking I should tell you something," he says.

"What kind of sad things?" I ask. I can see hesitation in his mannerisms.

"I'm thinking I will miss these lips when they're gone," he says, brushing his fingers over my lips as he says it. "I'm thinking I will miss these kisses, the touch of your skin, your warmth. I'm thinking one day they will go. I'm thinking one day I will no longer get to do this with you and it will make me sad."

I don't know what to say. His words render me speechless and that doesn't happen often. I would miss him too. "Will the thing you think you should tell me make me more sad?" I ask.

He shifts under me. "I think it could," he admits.

"Then don't tell me," I say. "I don't want to know. Not tonight."

He nods his head slowly. "Can we shower now?" he asks.

I nod back. We stand and I start the shower as I let the drain out to empty the bath. We wash and rinse mostly in silence. We turn to lighter bits of conversation as to not completely drown the evening in sorrow. We get out and dry off, then wrap the towels around us. We never put clothes on after. We simply walk to my bed and take the towel back off. I'm not even sure why we bothered wearing the towels the short distance we did except to soak up any extra moisture on our bodies.

I sit on the edge of the bed and let my towel fall in a c-shape around me. I lie back across my bed and Lucas does the same right next to me. He reaches for my hand and we lie here for a little while, staring up at the ceiling in silence. It's not awkward though. When silence falls over us it tends to be very comfortable and peaceful. This moment is no different. Our fingers are laced together and his thumb is drawing small circles on the back of mine. I like these moments most about us. These quiet, less obvious moments when we seem to be really connected, even without words or motion.

I feel Lucas shift onto his side and prop himself on his elbow to face me. He lets go of my hand and uses his index finger to trace over my lips. When he finishes, he traces over my chin and down my throat. He traces a line between my breasts and down to my belly button. He traces back up over my left breast and then my right. I know he likes doing this for the way it makes me squirm and arch. My reaction is half the fun for him. I keep my eyes closed while he does this. He traces over my collarbones, down my arms, over my hip bones. He touches everywhere except the place my body begins to crave.

"Lucas?" I whisper.

"Yes?" he answers.

"Can we pretend for just one night we are more than what we are?"

"What do you mean?" he asks.

"Make love to me," I say.

Without a word, he wraps his arms around me and kisses me deeply again, moving his hands into my hair. His lips kiss my jawline, my neck, my collarbone. His hands run down my back and he steadies himself over me. He pulls his face back from my neck and looks down at me.

"I've been making love to you for a while now," he whispers, and then I feel him pushing his way inside me.

I moan and wrap my arms around his ribs. I dig my fingers into his back. I kiss his chest. His movements are slow, deliberate, intense. I can feel everything. It comes over me in waves and I can't control my breathing or tongue anymore. I hold onto him tighter as I get closer and he can feel it so he slows down. He doesn't want me to go yet. He rocks back and forth with me. He kisses me and tucks my hair back as he cradles me. Then he starts again, faster and deeper and I'm climbing again. I feel his mouth on my neck and his breath in my hair. We're going together now and I feel him release as I do. He slows until he stops. He kisses my forehead and eyelids. He collapses into me and hugs me.

This might be my second favorite part of sex. The after. The cuddling. When your tired bodies are still tangled into each other and both of you are out of breath and everything is warm and slow and glowing. My chest is rising and falling rapidly and his arm is wrapped around my ribs just below my breasts and I know if we stay this way too long we will fall asleep just like this, sideways on the bed without a blanket or pillows.

"We have to move while we still have the willpower," I say.

"Who says I still have that?" he asks.

I laugh. "Okay, we have to move while one of us has enough to remind the other."

"Fine, but I want the record to show that I protested."

"And so it shall," I say.

We scoot ourselves up onto our pillows and wiggle beneath the blankets but keep the same positioning. We wrap ourselves back up into each other the same way and relax again.

"Dani?"

Lucas saying my name does something to me. It sounds right from his mouth.

"Yes?" I answer.

"I hope I've made you happy," he says.

His words are enough to make me cry but I keep it together. "You do make me happy, Lucas."

He doesn't say anything else. He kisses me gently and nuzzles his face into my neck. I feel him starting to drift off but his words have me wide awake. This is not what I had gone looking for. But it is what I found. And soon, it would be gone.

I stare up through the blackness at the crack in my ceiling and wonder what his ceiling looks like. His breathing had slowed and the rhythm against my own chest is so soothing.

There isn't much I can do now. Things will play out as they were always going to. I simply have to do my best to enjoy the rest of the ride. Nothing is forever, especially when you invest a great deal of time making sure your life is full of exactly that—always moments, never forever.

27

LUCAS

THE LAST FEW DAYS WENT BY IN A MOSTLY ROUTINE fashion. Dani's been keeping herself busy with work knowing I needed time for planning, so we haven't seen each other since that last night. The night she asked me to make love to her.

I have a few things to do today before I go to pick her up for the party and I'm actually nervous. Despite how comfortable I am with her, seeing her later actually makes me feel panicky.

I spent the morning confirming details with many of the guests. When to arrive, what to bring, what not to bring, if it was okay to bring a date, and so on. The questions felt endless.

I stop by the venue to finalize decorations. While normally most adult parties wouldn't have balloons and streamers, this one was special, so they wanted me to stop by and approve everything. The place looks exactly like I wanted it to. The back room has enough space for everyone to relax and dance. I even hope to steal a few away from Dani during the evening.

Now all that's left to do is walk two doors down and check on the cake. I stop briefly outside to check my phone.

Dani: I have no idea what to wear!

Me: It's your party, wear whatever you want!

Dani: I don't want to wear anything I have…

Me: So go get you something new, babe.

Dani: I don't know, should I?

Me: I want you to do whatever is going to make you feel your best tonight.

Dani: Okay, you're right. I'm going to go.

Me: Okay. Will you still be good for me to pick you up at seven?

Dani: Yeah, totally.

Me: Okay, see you then.

I tuck my phone back into my pocket and walk into the bakery where I'm greeted by a teenager at the register.

"Hi, I'm here to pick up an order for Kane," I say.

"Sure, just a second," she says, disappearing into the back. She emerges just a few moments later, accompanied by an older woman carrying a box.

"Mr. Kane? I have your order right here, I just need you to look it over and approve it," the older woman says. She opens the box and spins it open to face me.

I had opted for a three-layer vanilla cake with vanilla frosting and chocolate music notes and chocolate shavings decorated all over it. It's perfect. "Yes, this is great," I say.

The lady spins the box back around and closes it up.

I pay the remaining portion of the bill and take the cake out the front door and back over to the venue. Luckily, they had agreed to store it in their kitchen until the event so I didn't have to worry about transporting it further. This whole orchestrating a birthday thing really was quite tedious. I drop the cake off and repeat the motion of stopping outside to check my phone.

Elliott: Party still on?

Me: Yep, you still good to come?

Elliott: Yeah. The old lady can't make it but I'll be there.

Me: Cool.

Well, I can't say I'm not surprised. I expected him to flake by this point but maybe the fact that he was checking in meant he was actually going to show up. I check my watch. I have plenty of time to get home and get ready myself. I get into my car and plug my phone in so I can listen to Dani's playlists on the ride. The first song in the shuffle is "Hostage" by Billie Eillish and her sultry soulful voice seduces me much like Dani's mouth. Dani's lips could be very distracting in almost any situation.

I round the corner to my house and of course just as I'm settling into one mood, I'm hit with "Sabotage" by The Beastie Boys to completely throw me. Dani is good at that too. She keeps me on my toes if nothing else.

I park my car and make my way to my apartment, checking my mail on the way up. Jesus. Have I neglected it for a week or something? I stuff the stack under my arm and open my door. My apartment looks even more neglected than normal. Dishes are stacked in the sink and across the counter. Half empty glasses are on the table. Clothes are in piles on the floor in the hallway and my bedroom. I swear if I did have a wife, she'd divorce me for this shit. I check my watch again and think about cleaning up but decide against it. That just isn't my priority today; Dani is.

I meander through the piles to my closet to see if I even have anything clean to wear. Luckily most of my dressier clothes are still clean. I choose black pants, a white button-up shirt, and a black vest. I go over to my dresser and open my tie drawer. I pull out a few options before throwing all of them back in and opt to go a little more relaxed with no tie. I lay everything out on my bed and make my way to the shower. Showering, I found, was more a chore now when it wasn't with Dani. Because of that, I make them quick. In, wash, and out. No lingering whatsoever. No reason to. No wet naked lady to keep my attention.

I make quick work of the whole ordeal and dry off the same way. I wrap the towel around my waist and examine my face in the mirror. I would have liked a fresh haircut before today but I would have to manage without one. I run my hand up through my hair and that's when I see it. That's when it hits me like an anvil. I am wearing the wedding band.

I hadn't given it much thought until this moment. Dani is used to seeing it on me but everyone else? I don't want her to have to explain anything to her friends. And what about Elliott? I certainly don't need that kind of conversation after eight or more years. I stare down at my left hand intently. How would Dani feel? Is asking her wrong? Would she feel weird if I ask her opinion? I wish I knew the answer. We could pretend for one more day to be more than what we are.

I finish drying off, get dressed, fix my hair, and even have time to trim up my beard before it's time to think about leaving. I step in front of the full-length mirror in the corner of my bedroom and I'm pretty happy with the way I look.

Now is the moment of truth. I walk back out into the living room and grab my keys, wallet, and phone. I walk over to the dining room table and grab the enveloped with Dani's name written across the front of it.

All right, Lucas. Let's go get the birthday girl.

28

DANI

I LOOK MYSELF UP AND DOWN IN THE MIRROR FOR WHAT must be the seventy-eighth time and clench my fists on either side of me again. I tilt my head left to right and question whether a dress was the way to go. It is a special occasion, I suppose. I smooth my hands over the front of the short, black dress yet again. It falls a few inches above my knee. I adjust my boobs and the thin straps just to make sure everything will stay in place for the night. That's the thing about having boobs. They have a mind of their own and they tend to wander. Sometimes you have to rein them in a bit.

I check my makeup and reapply my lipstick and eyeliner. Lucas will be here any minute and for the first time since seeing him, I want to look as fresh as possible. My high heels will probably throw him off guard considering they are certainly not the usual boots or occasional Vans I adorn. For once in my adulthood, I could probably even pass for an almost-proper lady. I hear a knock at the door and immediately begin to shake. I don't know why seeing

Lucas suddenly makes me so nervous, but I take my time walking to the door just to calm myself. Not to mention, I'm out of practice in heels.

I open the door slowly to be surprised myself. Lucas has dressed out for the occasion too. His tight black pants certainly make the impression. All I think about doing is ripping the buttons from his white shirt and wearing it the next morning myself. And I must say, he looks stunning in a vest option. There isn't the typical Lucas smile across his face, however. Shock is a more appropriate word for what I see. His eyes search over what feels like every inch of me, starting low and working his way up.

"Oh, Miss Monroe. You'll have everyone eating their hearts out tonight, I can assure you," he says.

"You think so?" I ask, feeling my fists clench again.

"Oh, I know so. Stunning. You're absolutely stunning."

"Thank you. I should say though, the feeling is mutual," I say, looking him up and down to emphasize my point.

"Well, I can't accompany the birthday girl dressed like a slob, can I?"

"I suppose you're right, though I'm certain you would wear a potato sack and still be hot," I say, smiling and reaching for his face. I lean in and kiss his lips, lingering for a few moments, listening to his breathing get heavy against my mouth.

"I know we're supposed to be leaving now, but do you think we have time for just like a little something?" he asks, giving me the cheesy eyebrow lift.

"You mean a quickie?" I ask.

"Well, if you're going to be so crude, yes. A birthday quickie!" he says. His eyes glisten with that exaggerated birthday magic.

"Just because you stick the word 'birthday' in front of it doesn't make it better," I say. His entire demeanor is adorable.

His face grows sad, defeated even, in that fake exaggerated way again. "All right then," he says, hanging his head.

"I didn't say we weren't going to," I say, walking over to the kitchen counter, the surface nearest to us. I turn and lift myself up, sitting on the edge. I open my knees much wider than a lady would in a dress and call him over to me.

His expression changes in an instant. He goes from playful to hungry in the time it takes him to get to me. He kisses my mouth and neck while I unbuckle his pants and take him out. He reaches up my dress and runs his fingers over the front of my panties. I let out moans against the side of his face and feel him pull my panties to the side.

The next thing I know, he's already inside me, cradling my body against his, using only the smallest amount of counter for support. He kisses the tops of my breasts, up my neck, my lips.

"Happy birthday, baby," he whispers in my ear between the moans I release.

And it's shaping up to be that indeed. As soon as I finish, so does he and it's over as quickly as it started.

"We're pretty good at quickies," I say.

"Yeah, let's not make it a habit," he says.

"How come?" I ask.

"I prefer more time inside you," he says, biting his lip at me.

I can't disagree with him. But we do have somewhere to be. He buttons himself back up while I straighten out my dress and hair again. I check my makeup in the mirror and touch up my lips again.

"Ready to go?" I ask, grabbing my purse and sliding my phone into it.

"I sure am," he says, opening the front door for me.

We head down the stairs and out the front to his car. He opens the passenger car door for me too. Such a gentleman, even after a quickie. He walks around to his side of the car and we're off.

The place isn't too far away so we enjoy a silent ride holding hands until we arrive. I wait for him to come around and let me out. I step out onto the sidewalk and take a deep breath. Suddenly the idea of walking into a room full of people that are all there to pay attention to me doesn't sit well with me. Attention from one person at a time is enough to make me want to crawl beneath a cover. How will I avoid a whole room? I shake the thought from my mind. *It's okay. They came for me.*

Lucas seems to read my thoughts because he chooses to squeeze my hand and give me a little nudge. "Come on," he says. "Relax. What could go wrong?"

We walk in through the front door, his hand still in mine, and we make our way to the back room. Almost everyone who was on my list I gave him is already there. Quinn is chatting up who I can only assume is her new boyfriend from Tinder. My boss even managed to make it and has his arm around a woman. I will definitely have to find out who that is later. Robert is sitting alone the way I assumed he would. Some of my other co-workers and a few friends I'd made since being here had shown up too. I didn't recognize a few faces, so I think they might be Lucas' friends. I'm sure I'll meet them later.

I look around at the balloons and streamers and even though it's the part I thought I would hate the most, they actually look really amazing. I know they're what my mother had in mind for sure. Music plays over the room and I can't help but notice they are songs I would have picked. Lucas had really put so much thought into everything.

"Well?" he says, looking down at me.

"It's perfect," I say, smiling up at him. I wave over to Quinn who is waving frantically to me.

"Go join your friend. I'll get us something to drink and be right there," Lucas says, letting go of my hand for the first time since we left the car. He leans over and kisses my cheek before disappearing behind me toward the bar.

I make my way through a few people to Quinn.

"Dani!" she yells. She wraps her arms around me tightly and wiggles me back and forth.

"Hi!" I yelp back, trying my best to keep my balance.

"Happy birthday!" she exclaims.

"Thank you," I say, laughing, as she finally lets go of me.

She steps back and immediately runs her hands over her hair the way she normally does any time things get a little too exciting for a moment.

"Dani, this is my boyfriend, Jake. Jake, this is Dani, the birthday girl!" she says.

Jake is a tall and strapping man, though I expected no less.

He sticks his hand out toward me. "Nice to meet you, Dani. Quinn has told me so much about you," he says.

"I hope not too much," I say. I take his hand in mine and he starts laughing.

"I only mentioned the good stuff. All your secrets are safe with me," Quinn says.

"What juicy secrets are we divulging?" Lucas asks.

He had snuck up behind me and handed me a Rum and diet so skillfully, the conversation hardly skipped a beat.

"Just the birthday girl's secrets, of course. Don't want to steal the spotlight," Quinn says.

"Oh, then I'll be sure to pay special attention," Lucas says.

All four of us laugh and I feign annoyance, rolling my eyes. "Laugh it up, guys. I'll stab you all with a broken pencil."

Lucas slips his arm around me and kisses my temple. I grin despite my attempt to be ruthless.

"I have to say, Lucas, I've never seen her happier," Quinn says.

Lucas looks down at me. I shake my head at him.

"Is that so?" he asks.

"Don't listen to her, she's delusional," I say.

"Oh come on," she says. "You can't hide that glow."

She's probably right but denial is all I have.

"Well, I'll do my best to keep it that way," Lucas says, kissing my temple again.

I close my eyes feel his lips against my skin. "I need to go say hello to some other people, Quinn. I'll circle back, okay?" I say to her, hugging her and kissing her cheek.

"Go, girl!"

She turns her attention to Jake and we turn to scan the room for more people to chat with.

"Oh great! Hold on a second, okay?" Lucas says, leaving me there.

I watch him walk to the door where a woman is standing. She's older, like a grandmother's age. It's obvious they know each other. He walks her over to Robert and from the looks of it introduces them to each other. She sits down and I see Robert's face light up for the first time maybe ever since knowing him.

Lucas walks back to me and wraps his arms around me, looking pleased with himself.

"What was that all about?" I ask.

"Well, you told me about your neighbor Robert. And that nice lady is my lonely neighbor Stella. And I'm playing a little matchmaker at the moment." Lucas gives me his best evil grin.

"Oh my gosh, that's fabulous," I say. "I hope it works. We'll have to check in later." I take a sip of my drink and hear "Die Young" by Sylvan Esso come over the speakers. I begin to sway.

Lucas' face turns more serious as he watches me. "Let's dance," he says.

He leads me out into the center of the room, where the lighting is soft and staged for dancing. He slips his arms around me and I wrap my arms around his neck. We sway together in unison. I don't remember dancing with someone before this. Not at a school dance or for fun or in my adult life. No one had ever asked me to.

"Can I tell you something?" I say.

"Of course."

"This is my first dance. I just realized."

"Really?" he asks.

"No one has ever asked me to before."

"Well, I'm glad I fixed that. You can't go your whole life loving music, never being asked to dance," he says.

"I've danced on my own. Around the kitchen."

"That counts for something," he says. He presses his body into mine and rests his cheek against the side of my head.

I lean into him, and we sway like this, listening to this song about love, listening to this song about something we don't share.

As the song ends, I feel Lucas pull one hand away from my side. He begins to wave at the door behind me.

"Oh great, my brother is here! He actually showed up!" There is genuine excitement in his voice. "Wow, he hasn't changed a bit," he says.

"Great, do you want to go see him?" I ask, pulling away from Lucas and adjusting my dress.

"I'll just wave him over."

I look up at Lucas and he looks back down at me. Dancing to that song was probably the best gift I'd get all night. I know being able to meet his brother would mean a lot to him though.

"Oh, here he is!" Lucas says.

I turn and freeze. All the saliva drains from my mouth. I squeeze Lucas' hand without drawing too much attention.

"Dani, this is my brother, Marcus Elliott Stone. Most people call him Mark, I call him Elliott. Mark, this is who I've been telling you about. This is Dani." Lucas looks from my face to Mark's and back to mine.

"So nice to meet you, Dani," Mark says, putting his hand out to shake mine, as if we'd never met before.

I'm still half-frozen in place but starting to come around to what's happening. I mechanically put my hand in his. "Nice to meet you too," I say.

Mark squeezes my hand hard, shaking it up and down a few extra times before letting it go. Fuck. Of course. This is what happens in the city. Everybody fucking knows everyone. I feel my heart beating rapidly in my chest and try to smile normally.

"I'm so glad you could make it. It's been what, like eight years?" Lucas says, turning toward Mark but keeping his arm around me.

I zone out a little.

"I hardly recognized you, honestly," Mark says to Lucas. "If I saw you on the street, I might not even know who you are. When did you cut all your hair off?" He takes a sip of his beer.

"It's been a few years now," Lucas says.

Something about how he's speaking creeps me out more than normal. Mark was always a creepy guy, but something is extra off about him right now.

"If you'll excuse me, I'm going to go to the restroom," I say, loosening myself from Lucas' arm and smiling before stepping away from them. I need to walk away and think for a second.

Fuck, should I tell him? Mark is clearly fine not saying anything. But Mark is also the type that may actually be telling him right now after I've walked away just to be an asshole. I look back over my shoulder and they don't appear to be talking about anything serious so I seem safe enough for the moment.

I push the door to the bathroom open and walk all the way to the last stall. I lock it behind me and lean against the door, exhaling for what seems like the first time since I saw Mark's face.

What the fuck am I going to do?

MARK

THAT BITCH. THAT DUMB FUCKING BITCH. MY BROTHER?
Are you kidding me? I'm hardly able to concentrate on
what he's saying to me because I can't get over the fact that
Dani is right in the bathroom over there. All I want to do is
tell him. What's she doing with him anyway? None of this
makes sense.

Maybe, just maybe I can slip away. Like I give a shit about
Lucas anyway. The term "brother" barely exists between
us. We aren't exactly close. It's been eight years since the
last time we saw each other and let's just say it wasn't
exactly a lovely time then either. He was always jealous of
me. My father took him in and he didn't appreciate it at
all. His bitch mother wasn't even good enough for my
father.

I don't even know why I came tonight or why Lucas kept
pushing to mend this relationship. He's soft, that's why.
Focus, Mark.

I need to get away from Lucas and go talk to Dani. I have to. I can't just leave this alone. No fucking way.

"So where's the cake?" I ask Lucas.

"Oh, thanks for reminding me, I should get that set up while she's in there. I'll talk to you in a little bit," Lucas says, turning toward the door. He'd be gone long enough.

I move toward the bathroom and take a quick scan before pushing the door open and backing in quietly.

I told you, Dani. Nobody tells me no.

I HEAR THE BATHROOM DOOR SQUEAK OPEN AND SHUT again. I hear heavy footsteps walking slowly across the floor. I look out under the stall and the shoes are men's. *Lucas?* I open the stall door.

"What are you doing in here, Mark?" I ask, rolling my eyes.

"What's wrong? Not happy to see me, Dani?" he asks.

"I think we both know the answer to that," I say.

"You used to be happy to see me all the time. What changed?" he asks.

"Well, remember that time you were an asshole that basically tried to rape me? You were dead to me after that."

"Oh come on, you know you liked it," he says.

I try to walk past him and he cuts off my path to the door. "I'm not doing this with you, Mark. Let me out of here," I demand, trying to move the other way past him. He cuts me off again.

"Do you remember what I said to you, Dani?"

I roll my eyes again. "You spewed so much bullshit, Mark. Which time do you mean?" I ask. He lunges toward me and puts his hand around my neck, pushing me back. I lose my footing and try to regain it as he shoves me to the wall.

"I said you'd pay, Dani. I said no one tells me no. Remember now?"

"What the fuck, Mark? Get off me!" I yell.

He puts his hand over my mouth and pins me with his forearm, freeing one of his arms. "I take it your little lover boy doesn't know, does he? He doesn't know I've been inside you too, does he?"

I shake my head.

"Of course not," he says. "I wonder if he can taste me on you."

He laughs and I try to jerk myself free but he just slams me back into place.

"Where do you think you're going, birthday girl? I haven't given you your gift yet," he says.

I feel Mark's free hand slide down my side and reach the edge of my dress. I start shaking my head side to side.

"Hush now, we don't want to be interrupted," he says.

I feel his fingers running slowly up my thigh and he starts playing with the edge of my panties. My legs want to collapse. I feel sick. I can't believe this is happening. I can't believe no one has come looking for me. How long has it been? It feels like it's been at least an hour. Mark tilts his head down and smells my neck. I close my eyes. The worst part of my childhood is now replaying and I'm just as frozen now as I was then. I try kicking my legs just as I had the first time he did this. Mark pushes his body hard against mine, taking my breath away.

"You're not doing that again, love. I've learned my lesson," he says.

I keep my eyes closed, waiting for what he might do next.

"I'm going to enjoy this more than any of our other times together," he says against the side of my face.

I hear the bathroom door swing open behind him and my eyes shoot open.

"What the fuck are you doing?" Lucas' voice rings out, loudly, echoing in the small bathroom.

Mark reluctantly lets me go; not with haste or worry, just with a shrug of his shoulders and a laugh, like what he was just caught doing is no big deal at all. "Don't worry, man, it's not a big deal," Mark says, holding his hands up in front of Lucas.

"The fuck it isn't, Elliott," Lucas says.

I stand there against the wall, still half-frozen, attempting to wrap my arms all the way around my body to protect myself.

Lucas walks across the floor, getting in Mark's face.

"You sure you want to do this?" Mark asks, looking at Lucas.

"I've never been scared of you, Elliott," Lucas says. He rears back and punches Mark square in the jaw.

Mark staggers back and falls to his knees. He cups his jaw and gets back up. "That's fucked up, Lucas. Why would you be defending the honor of a slut like Dani anyway? Did you know I was fucking her before you? I bet you didn't."

Lucas looks at me and I can feel tears begin to stream down my cheeks. That's probably all the answer he needed. He nods toward me with assurance.

"I didn't think she was a virgin when I met her, Elliott. I'm not an idiot." Lucas crosses his arms and stares at Mark.

Mark looks at Lucas and then back at me. "Seriously Dani, I thought you only fucked married guys?" Mark says.

I stare at him, confused. "But Lucas is married," I say, my voice shaky.

"Is that what he told you?" Mark starts laughing.

I look at Lucas, more confused than ever. "What is he talking about?" I ask.

Lucas drops his arms. His face goes soft. "Dani, I was going to tell you…"

"Tell me what?!" I raise my voice. Is this actually happening?

"He's not fucking married. He never has been!" Mark yells.

Everything in my face drops. I don't even know what to say.

"Shut up, Elliott!" Lucas shoots his brother a look and then comes back to me again. "Listen, I can explain, but not here, not like this. I need more time than this," Lucas says.

"This is all we have, Lucas," I say. "What are we supposed to do? Just go back to the party like none of this is fucking happening?" I rub my temples. My god, this can't be happening. What the hell am I supposed to do? All those people.

Lucas looks at me again. "Dani, I…"

"No, Lucas. I can't do this. This is insanity. Tell everyone I went home sick or something, I don't fucking care. Tell them to eat the cake or whatever. I just can't be here right now." I push my shoulders back and step around Mark. I walk past Lucas to the door and pause before I open it. I take two deep breaths and exhale. I pull the door open and walk straight for the exit as fast as I can. I hear Quinn behind me calling my name but I don't look back. She'll understand later when I explain. I grab my purse from the front and make it out to the sidewalk without anyone trying to stop me.

That's when I feel it rising up inside me. The slow rumble that starts in the pit of your stomach. The chill deep inside your bones fueled by adrenaline and anxiety. I could be wearing five sweaters and I'd still be shivering. I call it the death shiver. Nothing I could do would stop it. It was made of fear and anger and pain. It had to go away on its own. Until then, I was a leaf in the wind.

I lean against a lamp post and steady myself. Part of me thinks I might puke. I close my eyes and take a few deep breaths.

After a few minutes, I stand back up and compose myself enough to walk. I dig into my purse for my headphones and put them in. I need music today like I've needed it my entire life. If anything, this reaffirms my reason for needing it. Tragedy. Fucked up tragedy strikes, and I turn to it. I need something angry, something angsty. I need to go back to hating the world and everything about it. That's what tonight did. Reminded me what I was and why I was.

I stop at the corner to wait for the light to change before crossing and look back toward the restaurant. Lucas didn't follow me. He didn't call me or text me and he didn't run after me. Part of me thought he might run after me. I should be used to that kind of disappointment by now. Fuck him. I shouldn't even care like this. Everyone has another side. Everyone has true colors. Tonight, I learned his.

The light flashes to the walker and I pick up my pace. I will put this night behind me. I will put this whole mess behind me. I will put Lucas behind me the way I always knew I would have to one day. Today just happens to be that day. I got the best gift I could. A life lesson. Happy birthday to me.

31

LUCAS

It's been eight days since Dani's party and she still hasn't spoken to me. The first two were radio silence. I thought it was best to give her a cooling off period, which also gave me time to collect my thoughts, to best figure out how to explain this monumental fuck-up to her. It isn't easy trying to figure out a way to explain a lie that has essentially defined nearly your entire adult life. A lie I choose to tell to perpetuate a lifestyle, by the way. Fuck. That sounds completely horrible.

On day three, I tried calling her but she didn't answer. I left a voicemail and waited three hours. I tried calling again and she pushed the hater button on me, sending me straight to voicemail again. I left another message and waited another three hours. I tried calling one more time but got no answer yet again. After that, it didn't seem like a phone call was going to work.

On day four, I texted her that morning begging her to speak to me. No reply. I waited a couple of hours and begged again. No reply. This pattern repeated itself for two days and yielded no results. On day six, I tried showing up at her apartment. She didn't answer the door and I felt like a complete fucking stalker just for doing it but desperate times and all that. I left a note pinned to her door as if maybe she weren't home, asking her to call me, but I knew damn well she was.

Yesterday, I tried having flowers delivered and drove by her apartment later to see them scattered all over the sidewalk below, her apartment window open, the curtain rippling in the breeze. Flowers were clearly not the way to go. Which brings me to this moment, sitting in my car outside of her work like a creep. I know she's working and I can see her through the window behind the bar. The last thing I want to do is go in there and accost her at work but she has to hear it. She needs to know what I need to tell her.

I get out of my car at a snail's speed and walk into the bar. She doesn't notice me as I make my way up to her part of the bar and take a seat. Then her eyes catch mine and all at once I am petrified.

"What are you doing here?" she snaps.

"I just need you to listen to me, please?" I say.

"I don't want to, Lucas," she says. "You're a liar. I know what those sound like."

I gulp. I can't deny her logic. "Just five minutes," I beg.

She rolls her eyes and exhales. "Five minutes. That's it." She exits the side of the bar and leads me out to the side alley where she takes her breaks. She leans back against the side of the building and crosses her arms. She is as far away from me physically as she possibly could be.

"Listen, Dani, I'm really sorry for how everything came

out the other night. Truly. I never wanted it to be like that. As for my brother, I don't think I can apologize enough for the way he acted. It's unforgivable."

"I've dealt with plenty of Marks in my life, Lucas," she says.

"Right," I say. I try gathering my thoughts as quickly as I can. "Still, it was deplorable. But that's not the point. And I don't care that you were with him before, I really don't."

"You think I care about what you think now?" she scoffs.

Another valid point. "Right, I'm sure you don't, I just wanted to make it known," I say. "What I came here to really say was well, okay, you know what? I'm just going to say it. I love you. Okay, Dani. I love you." I breathe.

Dani stares blankly at me, studying my face. "Is that a punchline?"

"What? No. I'm serious," I say. "I love you."

"Stop saying it," she says.

"Why?"

"Because your five minutes are up now," she says. She uncrosses her arms and shifts her weight to go back inside.

"Dani, wait, I'm serious here," I say.

"Just shut up, Lucas. People don't love each other. They hurt each other. That's what they do. There is no happily ever after storybook anything. There is no knight in shining armor. No prince to rescue anyone. My mother calls me a fucking princess and do you know what I got? I got a fucking whore mother, spent half my life in a closet, the other half in foster care until I aged out, and no one loved me Lucas. My first birthday party in my entire life and I'm nearly sexually assaulted and then, then the one man I think might actually care for me, well come to find out he's been lying to me the entire time I've known him. So don't tell me about love, Lucas. You don't get to love me now. You don't really love me. And even if you did, I wouldn't know how to let you." She takes a breath.

I can see her eyes brimming with tears and I know she doesn't cry in front of people. It was enough that she cried in front of people on her birthday. I'm not about to have it happen again right here.

"Okay, Dani. Okay. I'm going to leave. I don't want to hurt you anymore," I say. I tuck my hands in my pockets and put my head down.

She takes a few more deep breaths and regains her composure. "You don't have to worry for much longer. I'm leaving soon. The city I mean."

"What? You're moving?" I ask. "When?"

"A few weeks from now," she says. She straightens her apron and tucks her hair behind her ear.

"But that's so soon," I say.

"Yeah well, when your life falls apart, you sort of make an effort to get away from it fast," she says, shrugging. She opens the door to the bar and steps back in. "Goodbye, Lucas."

I stand there in the empty alley for a while, thinking about what she said to me. None of it was wrong. Too much of it was true, in fact. Except the part where she said I didn't love her. I hadn't been in love for a very long time but I remembered its taste. I remembered what it felt like flowing beneath my skin.

I don't know what to do, where to go from here. There are conflicting ideals in my mind. On the one hand, the old adage "if you love something, let it go" and on the other, "fight for what you love". Proof in and of itself that love is contradicting and downright treacherous.

I thought about Dani's pain. What growing up in her shoes must have done to her heart. The way it must have walled her off to feeling so much. The way it must have filled her with so much doubt and fear. I didn't blame her. I couldn't. She was a product of too many bad memories and lonely mornings. Could another person even begin to mend something so devastated? Or would that type of healing have to come from inside? Could it be both?

She doesn't want me around anymore, that much is clear. All that has happened has literally driven her to want to move away and I can't stand the thought of her leaving. I have to fix this. I'm not even sure about winning her over or back, but I have to make her stay here. I don't know how, but I have to think of something. I have to make her see.

I walk back into the bar and past her station. I don't look her way. I don't want to upset her anymore, and as much as I would have liked to have one more look at her, I knew she wouldn't want me to. I walk out the front door and back to my car. I have to go. I have to find a way.

32

CHARLOTTE

My Dearest Dani,

I was so excited to receive your call the other day after your birthday party but the excitement was cut short when you told me how it went. I wrote this letter to you as soon as I got off the phone with you so I could explain some things. I'm so sorry to hear it wasn't the best birthday. I wanted it to be so much more for you and I'm sorry I couldn't be there like I'm supposed to be to make that happen.

With that being said, I want to be honest with you. This is exactly the type of thing I attempted to avoid my entire life. And this is exactly the type of thing I wanted to prevent you from experiencing. I failed in that regard. It seems as though I've given you a lifetime of failures and disappointments. I never meant to do that. I never saw myself being that mother. I can't apologize enough for that.

So here it is, Dani. I'm a grown woman. I'm not going anywhere. I'm going to be here for the rest of my life. But that doesn't mean you have to be. That doesn't mean you have to stay in the city close to me with people who have wronged you. You don't have to suffer like that. Just go, Dani. Pack up your things and be free of them and me. There's no reason to stay. There's no reason to endure what you don't have to.

Go somewhere beautiful and start over, for the both of us. But for you especially. I can't give you a birthday present. I've never been able to. But I can do this for you. I can tell you what you need to hear. I can set you free. We shouldn't both be imprisoned.

I love you, Dani. I always have. I hope you know that but in case you've ever doubted it, please know it now. Go, my love, my princess. Go and live your life.

All my love,

Mom

33

DANI

IT'S BEEN FOUR DAYS SINCE LUCAS CAME TO MY WORK AND told me he loved me. He hasn't attempted to contact me again. I have read my mother's letter twice more since then and already packed half my living room and most of my kitchen into boxes. I put in my notice at work and informed the landlord of my intention to vacate so now it's just a matter of counting down the days.

Quinn was sad. She couldn't believe any of it. I explained the whole situation to her and her jaw dropped in shear disbelief. I didn't divulge such a truth to anyone else but I knew I could trust her with it. It wasn't the sort of thing you told just anyone but part of me wanted to make it known to the world so no one would fuck with me ever again. Trust me, no one will never fuck with me again.

I'm sorting through clothes in my closet, throwing several things in a pile to donate before moving and hear a knock at the door. I peek out my bedroom to look out into the living room and see if they knock again. They do, which means they are actually serious about having me answer and not just a door-to-door religious group or salesperson of sorts. I look through the peephole and unlock the deadbolt.

A man in a delivery uniform checks the tablet in front of him. "Miss Monroe?"

I nod in confirmation and he hands me the device and stylus to sign. "What is it?" I ask, looking into the hallway.

"It's actually several boxes, ma'am." He looks at the tablet when I give it back to him. "According to the manifest, there are eleven to be exact."

"Eleven boxes of what?" I ask. What on earth would be coming to me in so many boxes?

"And one envelope," he says. "I'll be back in a moment." He turns to go down the stairs.

Utterly confused, I watch as he and his partner go up and down the stairs six times each to bring them all up. The boxes are all the same shape and size. The delivery men stack them up neatly in my dining room and one hands me the envelope last. I turn the envelope over in my hand and see my name printed on the front. There's no return address. It feels too thick to be a single page. I open the envelope and unfold the pages.

Dani,

I know trying to see you again to explain all of this would be a mistake so I thought it would be best to try to write it all down. Maybe you'll just throw it away and that will be the end of it. But hopefully, you'll at least read the letter in its entirety so you'll understand me a little better. So you'll understand we are a little more alike than you realize.

Eight years ago, I was happy and in love. I was engaged to be married actually. For real. One day, I came home early and found my fiancé in bed with my bother. Yes, that's right. That's why we hadn't seen each other in eight years and that's why our relationship had been so strained. It turns out they had been seeing each other behind my back pretty much the entire time. I called off the engagement and severed all communication with Elliott.

A couple of years ago, my mother became very ill. Cancer. She fought hard but ultimately the cancer was stronger and she died with me by her side. I can't remember what excuse Elliott had for not being there and even though she was his mother too, he never really acted like it. He and his father always treated me and her like we were beneath them for some reason. I digress. Back to the point. She died. And before she did she begged me to try to make things right with him again. She reminded me that he was my only family now really, and that despite what had happened, I should be the bigger man since I'm the older brother. I promised her I would. For a little while, I didn't. But lately, it started to nag at me. I didn't want to break that promise to my mother, even after her death. That's when I started to try to find him.

Now, as for the lie. After catching them together, I went through a phase of swearing off women completely. Then I wanted something, just nothing serious. The trouble was, it was very difficult to be a single man and date casually and not eventually get a line of questions about why it couldn't be serious. Women always seemed to want more. Or they'd begin to develop a complex about themselves and I didn't want them doing that. Afterall, my decision was about me, not them. So I tried something. It wasn't right and I'm not proud of it. But I put my ring on. From when I was engaged. I went out and I told this woman I was married. I told her I couldn't invest into something serious. And she indulged me. Hell, I think she was even more into it thinking I was taken.

I'm not proud of this, Dani. But I faked being married so I could continue to have fun and never settle down. I didn't want to. I had no interest in it. At the same time though, I faked being married for the same reasons you only ever dated married men. To protect myself from what I knew to be inevitable: Pain. I knew one day someone like you would come along and completely crush me and I just had no interest in experiencing that ever again. My fiancé had done it and that was enough heartbreak for a lifetime as far as I was concerned.

None of that is an excuse for the pain I've cause you. None of that is a reason or rationale. But I am trying to make you understand just a little. And I hope you do, Dani. God, I hope you do. The day we had lunch together and you told me you only dated married men, I had a choice to make. I thought about coming clean right there in that moment but I was so scared about the idea of you not even giving me a chance after that, that I couldn't bring myself to do it. I had it in my mind the entire time to tell you the truth somehow, some way, and that moment just never came. I'm so sorry for that, Dani.

I know this letter can never take away the pain I've caused. This isn't me trying to ask you to give me a second chance or even forgive me. It's just a letter explaining my side.

You might be wondering what the boxes are right about now. I never got to give you your birthday present. And given what's happened, this seems even more important now. Dani, I've caused you so much pain. All I can remember you telling me is how much music helped you through all the painful times in your life. How music is what healed you. So maybe I can't heal you. I know that. But maybe what's inside these boxes can. They belonged to my mother. Needless to say, she had an extensive collection. She loved music the way you do. She gave them to me and they've sat in my living room collecting dust ever since. They need a home where someone will appreciate them, where someone will listen to them. Most importantly, they need a home where they can heal someone.

So that's all, Dani. That's all I wanted to say. Regardless of what you may think, I do love you. I never thought I would love someone again and even though this isn't how I would have liked it, at least I know I can do it. At least I know my heart isn't quite as broken as I thought it was. So I want to thank you for that. Thank you for showing me what love feels like again.

Take care of yourself, Dani. It's a strange and terrifying and beautiful world.

Love Always,

Lucas

I stand from my couch and look over at the boxes. I go to the kitchen to find the one unpacked knife I have and rinse it off. I pick the first box up from the floor and sit it on my dining room table, turning it around to face me. I carefully use the tip of the knife to slice across the top and ends. I flip open each flap of the top and remove the bubble wrap that has been tucked in.

I can't believe my eyes. No wonder the box is so heavy. Neatly filed in the box is vinyl record after vinyl record. Some are wrapped in plastic and look nearly brand new. Some look well-worn and well played. I flip through the titles, seeing Bowie, Elton, Joplin, Prince. So many great albums in one box. I shove the box aside and open the next one. Some of these albums I've never even heard of. Some of the artists too. Some are newer artists, classical music, The Beatles. If you could think of it, it was in here. I flip through the third box and then the fourth. I open the fifth box and there it is. The record player itself. It's old but has clearly been well taken care of. I pull the sides of the box away from the player and slowly lift it out of the bottom of the box.

I carry it into my bedroom, sit it on the trunk at the end of my bed, and then search frantically for the extension cord I keep in the top of my closet and plug everything in. I run out to the last box of vinyl I opened and flip through until I see the one I need. Sliding the record from the case, I return to my bedroom and lay it gently on the player and lift the needle to the edge of the record. The familiar sounds of "The Wolves (Act I & II)" by Bon Iver come through the speaker. I walk back into my closet and sit down with a thud.

I feel the familiar heat beneath my skin, the welling up. I try to fight it but I can't stop it. I feel the tears begin to fall from my eyes and run down my cheeks and lips and chin. I begin sobbing uncontrollably. I try to inhale but can't catch my breath and choke. I am full on ugly crying. I am a sopping ball of mess on the floor of my closet listening to a sad song from a beautiful gift from a beautiful man. I don't deserve his love. I don't deserve anything about him. I pat the ground around me. I pat my pockets until I find my phone. I don't know what else to do.

Me: Come here. Please.

All I could do now was wait. Hope. I sit back in the closet, letting Bon Iver play through to the next song. And the next. I look down at my phone. No response. Maybe it was too late. Maybe I had hurt him too much. Maybe his love had limitations. That would be understandable. The next Bon Iver song comes on and I hear my front door open and shut. I hold my breath, afraid to call out to him. I hear footsteps come through the living room and hallway and into the bedroom. I see the edge of his feet. He turns toward me.

"What are you doing in there?" Lucas asks me.

"I'm ugly crying," I say.

'Well stop it," he says.

"I can't help it," I say.

Lucas kneels down in front of me and leans forward, wiping the tears from my cheeks. "What's wrong, Dani?" he asks. He tilts his head at me, urging me to tell him.

"I just didn't see you coming," I say. "I didn't see you coming, Lucas."

I hear his breathing quicken. "I didn't see you coming either, Dani." He tips my chin up with his thumb and looks into my eyes.

"I don't know what to do now," I say.

"You could start by getting up out of the closet," he says.

I shift my weight and stand up, taking his offered hand. We stand together.

"That's better," he says.

I look around the room and press my lips together. My nerves had overcome me. I look at him. He moves toward me and puts his arms out. I wrap mine around him and he squeezes tightly.

"You looked like you could use a hug," he says.

"You're right," I reply. I look up at him from our embrace.

"Feel better?" he asks.

"Yeah, I think so. There's just one more thing," I say. I feel my hands begin to shake.

"What's that, Dani?"

I take a deep breath. "I love you too. And I've never said that before to anyone. So it terrifies me. But I do. And I tried not to. I tried to deny it. And when that didn't work, I tried ignoring it. But I can't do that anymore either. And this gift, Lucas. I can't believe it. I mean, these belonged to your mother. I'm truly just speechless about all of it. And I don't know what's happening or what can happen, but I had to tell you finally. I love you too."

I watch his face intently. It's nearly expressionless as he studies my face. I can't tell what he's thinking and that makes me even more nervous. He pulls his hand from my side and runs the back of his fingers across my jaw. He tucks my hair behind my ear. He places both hands beneath my jawline and looks into my eyes. He leans in closely, hovering for a moment, and then presses his lips hard against mine. I feel my body relax against his. I kiss him back, feeling his mouth move against mine. He pulls away and lightly presses his forehead against mine.

"I didn't see you coming, Dani. But I didn't know I was waiting for you either," he says. "I love you. I don't know what this can be but I know I want to give it a try. I know I want to find out. If you're willing, Dani?" He kisses my lips again and waits.

I breathe in sharply. I hear Kate Nash singing in my head and smile. "I want to see if we can be something," I say.

Lucas smiles and kisses me over and over again. He wraps his arms around me and picks me up so my feet aren't even touching the floor. He carries me over to the bed and lays me down. He lies down next to me and props himself up on his elbow.

I could get used to this. The way we are with each other. Perhaps I already had. Lucas was right. We didn't know we were waiting for each other. Not until we found each other. Not until it was here, daring us to be more than we were.

EPILOGUE

LUCAS

I ROLL OVER FROM MY SIDE OF THE BED AND INTO DANI'S back side, tucking my arm around her waist and pulling her into me. She wiggles herself back into me and lets out a small moan. Of all the ways I had woken her up over the past twelve months, I found this to be the one she enjoyed the most. Or at least the one she responded to the most.

She lays her arm over mine and nuzzles into me as deeply as she can. I put my chin into her neck and breathe in her scent. She smells like she always does. Coconut and a hint of peony. Or at least that's what she told me that flowery smell was.

"Good morning, babe," I whisper into her ear.

"Good morning," she murmurs, almost growling the way she does on the weekends before she has her coffee.

"It's Sunday, whose turn is it to make breakfast?" I ask.

We'd fallen into the routine of taking turns making break-fast for each other on Sunday mornings while the other was in charge of music selection and general entertainment for the chef.

"It's definitely your turn," she says with a groan. She isn't wrong.

"Do you want French toast or an omelet?" I ask.

"Definitely French toast." She turns to face me.

French toast is her favorite so it isn't exactly a competition. "With bacon?" I ask.

"When is 'without bacon' ever the right answer?" she asks.

"Good point," I say. I lie there looking at her perfect face. Her eyes are closed and it's this way that I find her most beautiful. First thing in the morning, with no makeup on, and no worry either.

"I can feel you staring at me, creep," she says.

"Want me to stop?" I ask.

"Never," she says.

I stare at her for a few minutes longer and then steal a kiss from her still lips. "One more question and then I'll go fix that French toast," I say.

"What?" she asks.

I reach under my pillow to retrieve the small box I had hidden there. She still has her eyes closed. I open the box and tap her gently on the shoulder.

She opens her eyes and they grow big and round and beautiful with a mix of excitement and fear like I imagined they would. "What are you doing?" she asks.

"Dani, we said we were going to see what this was, and I

think we both know what it is now. It's real, amazing, wonderful love. I can't imagine my life any other way. I love you and I love us. Will you give me the extraordinary pleasure of marrying me?" I hold my breath. Something like this with Dani, even as solid as I think we are, is a risk.

She looks at me and then at the ring and back at me again. "You're serious?" she asks, but not with doubt in her voice, or even fear.

"Deadly," I say, smiling at her.

She looks at the ring again and a smile begins to spread across her lips. "I'll marry you, Lucas," she says.

I exhale finally, sighing in relief. I take the ring from the box and slide it onto her left ring finger.

She looks at it on her finger and then turns and kisses me. She puts her hand around my neck and runs her fingers through my hair.

Some things are meant to change and some things are meant to stay the same. This is a fact of life.

"Does it fit? I measured your ring finger while you were sleeping like a creep so I hope so," I say.

"It's perfect," she says. "Can we do it in Vegas?"

"You want to get married in Vegas?" I ask.

"In a red dress," she adds.

"I shouldn't have expected anything traditional out of you," I say, laughing. "We can get married anywhere you want, wearing anything you want as long as you're mine afterwards.

"I'm yours now," she says.

"I need you to be mine, always," I say.

"Until death," she says.

"Maybe even after that," I say.

"Deal," she says.

She leans in and kisses me again, but this time she doesn't pull back. And she doesn't have to. I would be here for her. Forever. And I couldn't wait.

THE END

ACKNOWLEDGMENTS

I have so many people to thank, I hardly know where to start. So much goes into putting a book together. A lot less sleep, countless hours thinking about the plot, your characters, and the right words. Agonizing over the title and cover and worrying if people will connect. It's not a solo mission. It's never a solo mission.

Thank you to my lover, Chris, who works very hard every day to provide for our blended little family so that I can focus on writing more and more. You believe in me and push me even when I don't want to be pushed. Sometimes I don't like you for it, but I always love you.

Thank you to Jen Rogue and Christina Hart. I agonized about putting one of you before the other on this page and realized you're both so equally MY TEAM, that it didn't feel right either way. I would without a doubt lose my mind without the two of you in my corner every day. I love you both more than words can measure. We must all die at the same time please.

Thank you to my sister Brittany who loves and supports me the way only the best little sister in the world ever could. You show me every day that you can do and be whatever you want and you are a constant reminder to me that it's never too late to go on a new adventure. I love you immensely.

Thank you to all the bloggers and fellow authors and book community people! Your help and support through every release is undeniably important and immeasurably appreciated.

Thank you to every single reader who has ever picked up one of my books and fallen in love with my words. I cannot begin to express how much it means to me that you connect time and time again to what I write. You are what keeps me going.

ABOUT THE AUTHOR

Kat Savage resides in Louisville, Kentucky with her family of heathens. She's Slytherin, House Stark, and 99% sure her ancestors were pagan Viking Danes.

Kat Savage is a survivor of many ugly things and writes about them shamelessly in both poetry and novels. Join her reader group on Facebook—Kat's MF Savages—and be the first to know all her secrets.

Kat Savage would love it if you followed her Amazon author page and reviewed her work on Goodreads because it's very helpful to her as an indie author.

Kat Savages loves and adores you. You are important to her. Always.

Stalk her on social media

www.thekatsavage.com

thekatsavage@gmail.com